M000210370

WHATEVER HAPPENED NEXT?

DAVID B. LYONS

Copyright © 2023 David B. Lyons

The right of David B. Lyons to be identified as the Author of the Work has been asserted by him in accordance to the Copyright, Designs and Patents Act 1988. Apart from any use permitted under UK copyright law, this publication may only be reproduced, stored, or transmitted, in any form, or by any means, with prior permission in writing of the publisher or, in the case of reprographic production, in accordance with the terms of licences issued by the Copyright Licensing Agency. All newly-invented characters in this publication are fictitious and any resemblance to real persons, living or dead, is purely coincidental.
ISBN: 978-1-7398552-4-6

❀ Created with Vellum

To my readers.

Those wonderful, wonderful readers who embraced my second novel *Whatever Happened to Betsy Blake?* so much that it set me on the path to becoming a full-time author—a career I genuinely had always felt was out of reach.

To each of you, who bought that book, who reached out to me through social media about Betsy, who viewed the video link at the back of the book, who left a review for that book on Amazon, who emailed me to talk about Betsy and where she might be now... this follow-up novella is for you.

My thank you. To You. For gifting me this career.

I hope you appreciate where Betsy is now...

Let's go find out...

Love and gratitude forever,

David x

Home:
the most soothing word there is.

8:10

LENNY

Lenny exhales another elongated groan, then creaks his neck subtly, his stubble bristling against the pillow. His lay is uncomfortable. But comfortable enough for him to not have to move. He's been laying in the same position wide awake for over an hour now—awaiting his alarm's wail. Alarm isn't a clock for Lenny. Nor a vibrating iPhone. It's the cry of his twin boys. Jacob and Jared. Usually in unison. Almost always at the same time. For when one Moon twin wakes, the whole Moon house awakes.

Lenny has been wide awake because the day ahead was itching at his bald scalp. He reaches to scratch against the stubble of his temple, groans out another sigh, then finally swivels his shoulder — a slight swivel — slowly from his left to his right, then back again... with more force this time, until he is facing the empty side of the bed. The cold side of the bed.

'Why does she have to come today?' he whispers, patting at where Sally should be sleeping. 'Of all days.'

His next exhaled groan is released with such a bellow, that he sucks in a silence, suddenly, through his teeth, shutting himself up before cringing, anticipating his alarm's wail.

'Mammy!' Mammy! Mammy!' They both cry out. In perfect unison by the second call.

Lenny holds his eyes closed in frustration and scrunches up his nose, feeling a self-punch to the gut.

'That makes a change…' he whispers to the cold side of the bed. 'Me waking them up.'

It's not unusual the twins call out 'Mammy', over 'Daddy' first thing in the morning, but Lenny feels it ominous that was who they chose to wail out for today. Of all days.

'Hold onnn!' Lenny shouts, wiggling his bare torso out of his bedsheets, resting a knuckle of his spine against the narrow steel of the bedframe. He washes his hand over his shaved head, then kicks his two legs out of the sheets, shuffling his feet into the fur-lined slippers he had stepped out of to get into that bed some nine hours previous. He heaves himself to a standing position with a middle-aged groan, then stretches both arms towards his ceiling, his alarm's wail growing in volume.

'Mammy! Mammy…!'

'It's Daddy,' he yawn-shouts back, mid-stretch. 'I'm comin'. I'm comin'.'

The cries continue as Lenny shuffles his milky, pale, body — naked save for the fur-lined slippers and a pair of overly-tight H&M-emblazoned boxer shorts — out of his dated bedroom, across the squared carpeted landing, and into the twins' star-glowing bedroom. He strides the length of their twin beds, then stretches for the dim lamp that stands between them, pulling at its string. As soon as the room turns yellow, the cries for 'Mammy' fade to heavy gasps of excited, sharp inhales and exhales.

'Mornin' boys,' Lenny says, kneeling between the beds. 'You sleep well?'

He turns to Jared first. As usual. Jared slightly shows a tooth. But he's not smiling. Rarely is. Lenny winks at him, then turns to Jacob, his head tilting so that their eyes meet square on. Sometimes Lenny can tell, just by this first glance in the mornings, whether or not Jacob will be tuned in for the day. Not today. Not yet anyway.

Lenny thins his lips, wondering if Jacob remembers today is the day she is coming. Though if he had remembered, he likely would have said it by now.

'Where's Mammy?' Jared asks from over Lenny's shoulder.

Lenny continues to stare at Jacob. To see if he will answer the question his brother just posed. To see if he remembers... Really remembers... But Jacob remains silent. Mute. Staring not at his father, but through him.

'She's coming later today. Remember?' Lenny finally says, nodding his head. He then reaches a clawed hand to both of their stomachs and begins to squeeze. 'Now come on, you two,' he says, tickling them. 'Time to get out of bed.'

He relieves them of their excitement by letting go, and then rips back their duvets, exposing their matching red and grey-striped pyjamas. Jared and Jacob have always dressed the same. Day and night. Have done every day since they were born. Sally insisted on it.

Jacob gets to his feet slowly, stretching his arms to the high ceiling of his bedroom, mirroring how his father rises most mornings. Then Jared stands by slapping his feet to the thin carpet, following the exact same ritual—as if the evolution of man plays out in reverse in the Moon household every morning.

When all three Moons are standing in the tight space between the twin beds, it is evident Jacob is taller than Jared. But mostly because his stoop isn't as pronounced as his brother's. Soon enough, they'll both be taller than their father, though. Unusual for nine-year-olds. Sally used to wonder why they were so tall, when her side of the family tree was as miniature as the Moon family tree. She used to say, 'My uncle Bruce is tall. Maybe they get it from him.' Lenny never had the heart to tell her the twins were tall and bulky for their age because of their condition.

'Right, you two take turns having a pee in the small bathroom, and I'm gonna run downstairs to make breakfast. Remember, do not use the main bathroom. Use the small one next to your bedroom. Do you want eggs?' he says pointing at Jacob. Jacob nods once. 'Eggs?' Lenny says, turning to Jared. Jared does exactly as his elder twin just did. He nods. Once. He — more often than not — mirrors Jacob. That's why Lenny always asks Jacob first. It makes things easier if they both agree.

'Me too. I'm gonna have eggs,' Lenny says, pacing his milk-white skinny frame out of their bedroom. 'Make sure you wash those hands after you pee, you hear me..?' He doesn't get an answer. Not even an audible exhale which can usually pass as an affirmative in the Moon household. So, his slippers stop dead on the carpet, and he spins on the spot, his finger pointing again. 'Jacob, you hear me? Make sure you and your brother wash your hands before you come have breakfast. And remember, go to the small bathroom.'

Jacob nods.

'Yes, Daddy,' he says.

'Yes, Daddy,' Jared echoes.

Lenny spins back around, paces out of the twins' bedroom and strides across the squared-landing before pushing his bedroom door open with a slap. While the twins are shuffling their way out of their bedroom, Lenny reaches for the back of his door, unhooking his grey bear-skinned dressing gown before slipping his arms into and then tying it at the front.

He farts as he shuffles back across the squared landing,

causing his two sons to giggle just as they're entering the small bathroom.

Lenny cackles at their laugh and, as he is stepping his fur-lined slippers carefully, side-foot-by-side-foot, down the stairs, he stops all of a sudden, holding his eyes closed... breathing the moment in. Moments like this were rare in the Moon household. Lenny hadn't heard his own laugh in quite some time.

'Make sure you wash your hands!' he shouts back up the stairs.

He winces a little after shouting that, then grips the banister tight, another self-punch jabbing at his gut.

'Fucking idiot,' he whispers to himself, before jumping off the last step. 'Ruining the moment by giving them another instruction.'

He shuffles his slippers down the brown floorboarded hallway before chicaning into a kitchen that still looked fresh and new to Lenny. Even though it had been eighteen months since he had had it refurbished. The kitchen was one of only two rooms Lenny had invested money in.

He reaches for the cream kettle, sweeps it towards the sink and fills it before swinging back around, placing it on its cradle, and flicking the switch downwards. As the kettle begins to rattle, he rubs his two hands together, before shuffling his way out of his brightly-lit kitchen, back into his floor-boarded hallway, where he pauses on the spot, squinting... listening out for the boys above him. When he hears one of them peeing, he swivels and stretches for the dented, oval, bronze doorknob. Which he snatches at... and then pushes forward to begin his descent to the basement. Betsy's basement.

FIVE YEARS AGO

BETSY

There were pink and white balloons all around the door. In an arch shape. And every table inside the room had a pink or a white balloon sellotaped to the top.

There were cameramen and camera women inside that room. Fourteen of them. I counted. And there were six members of two separate police forces. Three from Ireland. And three from Wales. Twenty people in total. The most I've ever seen. That keeps happening. That happened yesterday, too. Three times. First, when three people walked down the steps of my basement and told me they were going to bring me 'home'. My elbows immediately started shaking. And I felt like a character in one of my books. I still feel like a character in one of my books. Those three brought me to a police station where I met five different officers in one room at the same time. A new record. They spoke to me for a long time. A long, long time. Then they sent me to two hospitals. A small one at first. Then a bigger one. I slept in the bigger hospital last night. Well, they left me alone to sleep when the sky went black outside. But me and Bozy didn't sleep. Not really. Because I kept feeling like I was a character in one of my books. As if nothing was real. Except the tests. They definitely felt real. Really, really real. They did seven different tests on me while my elbows were shaking. They wouldn't stop shaking. They did body tests. Throat tests. Blood tests. Pee tests. Poo tests... Then two people in suits sat down beside the bed and asked me lots of questions. Lots and lots of questions. For a long, long time... Until they all left me and Bozy alone... to sleep.

Eight people came into that room all at the same time this morning. I counted them. The one in the long white coat gave me pills and a plastic cup of water to take. And another in purple pyjamas put something in my arm that was attached to a hanging bag. I keep wondering if me feeling like I am a character in one of my books is because of what they put into my body. Down my mouth. Into my blood. My brain.

They gave me a breakfast that I said I didn't want to eat. But I did eat it. I had to. My belly was empty. After breakfast, they gave me new clothes to wear, then I was put in the back of a police van much like the one I'm sitting in now and brought me to a small airport. Three policemen and me then got onto an aeroplane that flew us to another small airport. That definitely made me feel like a character in one of my books. And it made think that me feeling like a character in one of my books was because of all they put inside me at the big hospital. Especially when they told me who I was going to meet. That's when I really felt like a character in a book.

When the plane landed at the other airport, the three police officers walked me down two long corridors, and then into the room with all the pink and white balloons inside it. The room with twenty strange faces. Fourteen camera men and women. And six police officers. A new record.

When they eventually snatched the door with the balloons all around it open, I remember squinting at first.

She was smiling really wide, running across the blue carpet towards me. He was staggering behind, squinting as much as I was.

My mom squeezed me tight and shrieked something into my ear. But I can't remember what it was she said. Because I was too busy staring at him, stumbling towards me.

When he got close I saw a bit of myself. A tiny, weeny little bit. Across his eyes. No, his nose. Definitely his nose. The bridge of his nose. As if the bullseye of his face is the same as mine. But the bullseye only. The rest of his face is wrinkled. And worn. And old. Really, really old. Older than Dod.

He reached an arm around me, tight, then went to put his other arm around my mom, but stopped himself, and instead, dropped it to the side of his long, brown coat. The cameras clicked and flashed while we hugged for a long time. A really, really long time.

'I thought you were gone for good, Elizabeth,' he finally said when the cameras had stopped flashing and clicking. I remembered *his* first words to me. Because he said them more calmly than my mom had screamed hers. I was still feeling like I was a character in one of my books. But during the hug, I remember my elbows shaking. Really shaking. As if they were never going to stop. And I wanted to cry. I needed to cry. Because Dod was gone. Dod was dead...

When the hug ended, we were asked to stand in a line — my dad on one side of me, my mom on the other — to stare at the camera men and women while they called out our names. My eyes were wet. But no tears fell. I know they didn't. I kept them all in. When the clicking and flashing stopped, everyone in the room — the fourteen camera men and women, and six police officers — began to applaud. Applauding me. As if I had done something. The noise was horrible. And my elbows shook again. I just wanted to hug Bozy tight. Really, really tight.

One of the Irish policemen made a long speech, and then everybody applauded again. I didn't applaud. I didn't move. In case one of the tears would fall. Then, a policeman came over and asked if we would like a lift home.

Home.

To where the police van has just pulled up outside. I stare out the back window, up at the giant block of flats staring down at us. And I already know I don't want to go up there. Not because it's so high, when I live below. But because I don't feel as if I am ready to be alone with these two anymore than I've already been alone with them in the back of this van.

'Now tell me,' my dad said, his voice so much weirder than Dod's. We were only in the back of the van one minute when he asked this. 'Did he touch ya? That Blake guy? Did he ever touch ya?'

'Jesus, Clyde,' my mom said. She said it in a whisper. But it was like a whisper shout. I only caught their faces when the daylight from the window would shine on them. Even though they had hugged me, and we stood in line for photographs in the room with all the balloons in it earlier, I didn't look at them. Not really. I couldn't look at them. Because the tears would fall. 'We've only just got her back. Give her a chance—'

'No!' I said, talking over my mom. 'He never touched me.'

I glance up at her now, even though her face is not lit by the window. She looks scared. And I begin to think that her scared is different to my scared. Her scared is seeing me again. My scared is not seeing her again. Or my dad again. My scared is Dod. Dod's dead. He died a day and a half ago. And now I'm staring out the back of a police van, looking up as far as I can see.

I have a feeling my mom and dad are both staring at me now that the policeman has stopped. But they don't say anything. They haven't really said anything since I shouted, 'No! He never touched me' to my dad. As soon as I said that the back of the police van fell silent. I love silence. But it wasn't a nice silence.

I squeeze my eyes shut, trying to soak the name 'Clyde' into my mind after my mom whisper-shouted it at my dad. But I don't know that name... Do I? *Clyde? Clyde? Clyde?* I don't even remember it from any book I've ever read. *Clyde?*

While we listen to the footsteps coming around the back of the van towards us, I stare up at her again. Realising I don't know her name, either. I didn't ask. Not in the hour we spent in that room full of pink and white balloons, and not in the twenty-minute drive over here. To this giant block of flats.

Her eyes meet mine, for a split second, before the back doors of the police van clang and clatter open, drowning the three of us in daylight.

It's the first time I notice that her hair is a thousand different shades of grey. Her face isn't as wrinkly and worn as my dad's. But her eyes look sad. And heavy. Really, really heavy.

When she steps out of the van and into the daylight and looks around at me, I notice a bit of me in her. A small bit. In the thinness of her lips. Thin lips that don't smile. Like mine.

She hugs me as I step down towards her, gripping me tight while the giant block of flats stares down at me from over her shoulder. She feels more relaxed in this hug than the long one she gave me earlier when the cameras were clicking and flashing.

'You've no idea how much I've dreamed of this moment,' she says.

I don't say anything to her. I don't know what to say...

When my dad staggers out of the van behind us, making a clanging noise, he begins to rub my back. It makes my elbows shiver. Again.

'Yeah, I've dreamed of this moment so much, too, Elizabeth,' he says.

'Betsy!' I say, my mom still squeezing me.

'I used to call you Betsy,' he says. His voice is all husky. And it's not very nice. 'Your mom never liked it.'

'Oh, shut up, Clyde!' my mom shouts right next to my ear.

My elbows shiver faster.

'I'm just sayin',' my dad says, still rubbing a circle into my back. 'I dreamed of this moment, too. Kept dreaming of it. I barely slept for six whole years.'

'Six?' I say, leaning my chin off my mom's shoulder.

My dad walks around my mom and stares at me. When he leans closer I notice his really thin moustache for the first time. It's thin and wiry. And yellow.

'I know. You were gone for seventeen years. And I only didn't sleep for six. Well... I'm sorry to say, Betsy,' he says, his yellow moustache waving. 'But I gave up. I had to. I had to move on. For my own...'

He stabs a finger to his temple.

'I never gave up,' my mom says.

'Yes you did!' my dad says. 'Let's not lie. We all did. We never thought this day would come. Let's not kid ourselves.'

'Shut it, Clyde, Jesus Christ!' my mom shouts.

I start to feel like a character in one of my books again. As if this isn't real. It can't be real. I just want to blink my eyes, and when I open them, I am back in my basement, and Dod is walking down the steps, bringing me a brand-new book.

My shoulders begin to shake like my elbows. And a sob jumps from the back of my face; from the back of my throat; the back of my nose. Suddenly my cheeks are soaked wet.

'Ah, look at you, getting all emotional,' my mom says, squeezing me tighter. 'I spent the whole night crying,' she says into my ear. 'As soon as we got that call last night telling us you'd been found, I was in floods of tears. Tears of happiness. That's all you're crying, ma love,' she says. 'Tears of happiness.'

She's wrong. I'm not crying tears of happiness. I'm broken. Heartbroken.

I swipe the tears from my cheek and suck up my nose, but more tears fall. My dad leans closer to give me another one-armed hug... And in a moment of crying about losing Dod, I can smell Dod. On my dad's warm breath from under his yellow moustache. Not good Dod. Bad Dod. The Dod who drank too much wine.

I whiff through my lips and lean way from my dad. Which makes me feel bad. Because his wrinkles get wrinklier and I know I hurt his feelings. I don't like hurting feelings.

'It's alright, ma Betsy,' he says, stretching around me to rub another circle into my back. 'This is a lot for you to take in.'

I close my eyes and try to like his touch. But it doesn't work. I don't like it. At all. I want him to stop. I need him to stop. But I can't pull away from him. Not again.

'Come on, ma love,' my mom says, linking her arm inside mine, jerking me away from my dad's breath. 'Let's get you up to this flat.'

'Hold on!' A policeman shouts from behind us. The three of us spin round to face him. 'I'll be dropping by tomorrow morning after breakfast. We're taking you, Betsy, to Glan Clwyd Hospital. Just to run more tests.'

I thin my already thin lips at the policeman, and he nods at me before turning around to grab my life from the front of his police van. I walk towards him a little, while he wheels it towards me.

'Thank you,' I say, taking the handle from him.

I am always polite. All of the characters in my books that I like are polite. The policemen nods again, and then I turn away to face the flats.

'Jeez,' my dad says. 'Where are ye living now?'

I look at my mom as I wheel my life over the cracks in the pavement behind me, the three of us walking towards grey, concrete steps.

'I've been here almost seven years, Clyde,' she says, tutting. Then she grips me around the arm tighter, leading me towards the concrete steps. I don't like the look of the concrete steps. My elbows begin to shiver. Again.

'What floor you on?' he says, stopping walking so he can look up.

'Sixth!' my mom shouts back over her shoulder.

'Sixth? Fuck me, Meredith,' he says. His voice is all gruffly and horrible.

When we reach the grey steps, I stop to press the handle of my suitcase down. But I don't lift it. I can't lift it. Not yet. Instead, I stare at my mom's face. At her thin lips. Her thin lips that never smile.

'Meredith?' I say, squinting at her.

'Yes,' my mom says, her head nodding. 'Did you forget? Did you forget our names, Betsy?'

'Huh?' I say, shaking my head.

'Did you forget our names, Betsy? What do you remember.... What do you remember about us?' she asks.

My elbows begin to shiver faster. Just as my dad catches up with us. Maybe it's him. Maybe it's the cold. Maybe it's everything else. I bend down and begin to unzip my life, before reaching inside to grab him from where I left him—sleeping on top of the books. I squeeze Bozy to my shoulder tight. Really, really tight. Then the tears begin to fall down my cheeks again.

'Betsy,' my mom says, putting her hands on my shoulders. 'Betsy... what do you remember about us?'

I squeeze Bozy tighter, then I sob; my shoulders shaking with my elbows. My face soaked wet.

'I don't remember anything,' I say.

8:35

LENNY

When Lenny first moved into 166 South Circular Road, a narrow patch of the basement had been freshly painted a very pale sky-blue. He liked the colour so much, that he purchased the same paint and finished the job himself. The basement, aside from the kitchen, was the only room the Moons had invested money in.

He painted both the ceiling and walls of the basement pale blue, then complemented that lightness by opting for a gloss-white Ikea desk that he would stand on its highest setting under the curve of the ceiling on the stairs side of the basement —where Betsy's bed used to lie. His oversized office chair was ill-fitting for the desk, but he chose it to be the throne from which he would work simply because it offered his spine the most comfort out of all of the chairs he had tested during a long Sunday afternoon in Ikea with Sally and the twins. He purchased the shiny-white filing cabinets that line the opposite wall of the basement that day, too.

His choices of office furniture made the basement an even tighter space, but it sure was a lot bigger than the five feet by five feet office Lenny had rented in Tallaght when he first became a private investigator.

While the twins were dipping bread soldiers into the yolks of their boiled eggs in the kitchen above him, Lenny was skimming over paper-clipped sheets of work notes, ignoring his mobile phone as it buzzed incessantly against the gloss-white Ikea desk. He was flicking through the notes he had written in bed the previous night on the Alan Dennings case. Alan was a fifteen-year-old moody schoolboy who had had an argument with his father in their Greystones mini-mansion two days prior, then vanished without a trace. Lenny already knew the conclusion to this case, even though it had yet to be solved. Alan will, he was certain, end up being found safe and sound, hiding out in a friend of a friend's house before being forced by authorities to return to live with a father who is bullying him, likely because he, too, was bullied by his own father. Lenny knows that story inside out. That story defines the missing person cases Lenny has grown his business on.

His face had appeared on the front page of the *Irish News of the World* when Betsy Taylor was found five years ago, under the banner of an 'exclusive' story penned by notorious journalist Frank Keville. It was that story that transitioned Lenny's business from an investigative practice that solved insurance claim complaints, into a company that investigated more serious cases within a week. Serious cases such as missing persons, or even the odd cold case murders on rare occasions—when Lenny got lucky. His clients were, for the most part, happy with his efforts; happy to pay him the hourly rate he had quadrupled in the wake of the Betsy Taylor case. His career could have taken him further, though. A lot further. Literally. The need for investigators of missing people cases operating in Europe is infinite given the astronomical wave after wave of people-trafficking. Five thousand humans go missing every month through Europe, meaning there are so many cases that investigators simply can't give them the time required. As a result, Lenny has been called upon to solve cases through different neighbouring countries over the years. But he's had to turn the opportunities down. He had to be close to home. For Sally. And for his boys.

He blows out his cheeks as he drops the paper-clipped sheets to his desk before stretching across that desk to snatch at a white, wooden-framed photograph. Sally's smile looks genuine in the moment, basking in the warmth of a double hug from her twins. A genuine smile was rare for Sally. That's why Lenny framed this photo for his desk.

'Why does she have to come today?' he whispers to the photo. 'Of all days.'

He sighs again as he places the frame back to his desk, then he scoops the Alan Dennings paperwork up and spins on his oversized office chair, pulling open one of the bright-white filing cabinets. As he's stuffing the paperwork inside a cardboard folder, he hears a heavy creak from the floorboards above.

'That you, Jacob?' he calls out.

'Daddy!' Jacob shouts, his voice echoing down the brown, wooden basement steps.

'Daddy's down here,' Lenny shouts back.

'Daddy, Daddy,' Jacob says, repeating himself as he pulls the basement door open. 'Finished breakfast, Daddy.'

Lenny sighs, silently, into his own chest, then glances up at his son shuffling, slowly and side on, down each creaking step. The steps were the only part of the basement Lenny hadn't brightened. He hadn't thought to.

'Careful, Jacob,' Lenny calls out. 'You know I don't like you coming down here.'

Jacob doesn't answer. He can't answer. Not while he's concentrating on gripping his thick fingers to the banister.

When he finally reaches the bottom, he looks up at his dad and smiles his buck-toothed grin. But that's all he does. He doesn't say anything. He doesn't have anything to say. If he did have the intention of shuffling down the basement steps to say something to his father, it sure had been forgotten during the duress of the descent.

'Has Jared finished his breakfast, too?' Lenny asks.

Jacob inhales as if to say something, before exhaling a huff. Then he just shrugs his shoulders when the huff has fully deflated from him.

'You're supposed to be looking after your brother, Jacob,' Lenny says. 'You're the oldest. And the wisest. You know that.'

Jacob scratches his chin, then reaches both arms around his father's waist and squeezes him tight against his own body.

'I love you so much, Jacob,' Lenny says, resting his stubbled temple to the top of his son's thick mop of jet-black hair.

The mobile phone buzzing again against Lenny's desk stirs Jacob from the hug, and he releases his grip to cure his curiosity.

'Gwandad,' he says, lifting the phone from the desk, showing his father a portrait of Sally's father lit brightly on the vibrating screen.

'Yes, Jacob... I know it's Grandad calling. He's been calling most of the morning. Today's the day, isn't it? Don't you remember?'

The phone stops buzzing in Jacob's hand. And Grandad's face disappears, showing Jacob a mirror image of himself in the blacked-out screen. He places the phone back to the desk, then turns to his father as if he's about to say something. Only he doesn't. He doesn't even blink. He just sucks in a deep inhale, before slowly allowing it to deflate from him.

'You okay, Jacob?' Lenny asks.

'Talk to Gwandad,' Jacob says. He picks the phone back up and walks it to his father.

'We'll be talking to Grandad later,' Lenny says, palming the phone and then shoving it into the deep pocket of his grey dressing-gown. 'Don't you remember, Jacob? What's happening today?'

'Gwandad,' Jacob says, patting his hand against the pocket of his father's dressing-gown.

'We'll be talking to Grandad later,' Lenny says. 'We all will. We'll be talking to Grandad later.'

Jacob huffs and puffs, before tucking his chin into his thick neck to stare downwards; down towards his webbed feet as they sprout from under his flared grey and red-striped pyjamas.

'Look,' Lenny says. 'Everybody's calling me. Because today's the day, isn't it?' He shovels his wiry hand into the pocket of his dressing-gown and pulls out the phone, swiping his forefinger across the screen. 'Look, Jacob,' he says. 'Everybody's calling me. I've had eleven missed calls this morning. Five from Grandad, three from Barry and Eleanor. Your auntie Debra has called twice... and...oh,' Lenny says, tilting his chin on top of his son's mop of thick hair. 'Celina has called.'

Jacob leans his head away from his father so he can stare up at him, just as Lenny is stabbing a finger to the screen.

'Hul-ho,' she finally says, her voice melodic, her accent so comfortingly familiar as it crackles through the speakerphone that it causes Jacob to offer a toothy grin.

'Hey, Celina,' Lenny says.

'So, today's the day, huh?' Celina says.

FOUR AND A HALF YEARS AGO

BETSY

I grip the newspaper tight, to tear it into pieces... but I stop myself, and, instead, drop it, crinkled, to my lap before slapping both hands to my face.

'Uuuugh,' I scream, hurting my throat.

'I've been telling you all about him,' my mom says.

I take one hand from my face, and hold it up to her, to stop her. To stop her talking. And talking. And talking. And talking.

Her sixth-floor flat has three bedrooms. A stepfather. Bryn. And two stepbrothers. Both teenagers. Callum and Daryn. The two of them just stare at me when we are in the same room. But why wouldn't they just stare at me? They had to share a bedroom with each other to give their miracle step-sister her own space when she finally came 'home'. That's pretty much why I moved out of this flat on the sixth floor of Bracken Flats after two months. Well, it was to do with that, but also mostly because my mom would just not stop talking. And talking. And talking. And talking.

I had no other choice. I moved to Leeds to live with my dad and his fiancée, Winnie, in their small house in the middle of a long street. When somebody is a fiancée in a book, it's normally all romantic. But my dad and Winnie's engagement isn't romantic. She says she doesn't want to get married. Because she would lose twenty pounds a week on the dole. My mom hates Winnie. She doesn't hide it. In fact, from long before I was found, my parents had hated each other. My mom tells me everything. She had found out about my dad's affair with Winnie six years after I had been taken. My mom's not sure how long their affair had been going on but thinks it might have been from the very beginning. Winnie Ratcliffe was a stranger on the internet, from Leeds — who anointed herself as the chairperson of the Elizabeth Taylor Search Fund two weeks after I was taken and would begin visiting my mom and dad's house in Wales to help find me. I only have my mom's word for it all, of course. Dad and Winnie don't talk about how their relationship started like my mom likes to. My dad and Winnie don't really talk about anything really. They just drink warm cans of beer and watch TV all day. And all night. Which is why I prefer it in their small house on a long street in Leeds. I prefer the not talking.

'You can't go back to live there now,' my mom says, pointing at the crumpled newspaper on my lap. She is standing in the doorway of Callum's bedroom. The room I slept in for the first two months of my being 'home'. Or tried to sleep in. I spent almost every night of those two months crying into the pillows of the bed I am sitting on the edge of now. I still think about Dod all of the time. I just don't cry when I think about him all of the time. Not anymore. My eyes ran out of tears in the first two months lying on this bed, I think. I don't remember crying myself to sleep in Leeds. It makes me wonder if I will cry every night if I come back to sleep in this room again. That's if she lets me sleep in this room... I hope she does. Even though I don't like this room. It's all cream. Cream everywhere. Cream walls. Cream duvet. Cream pillow. Cream carpet. There is a bit of colour when Callum lives in it, because he has posters of football players in red stuck to his walls. They're players for a team called Wrexham. Mom says they play their football matches an hour's drive away from the flat. Fifteen thousand people go to see them there. Thinking of fifteen thousand people all together makes my elbows shiver.

My mom wheels my life into the same cream bedroom it lay in the corner of for the first two months of my being 'home' and looks at me. Everything I own is in that suitcase. But mostly books. Books is all I ever want to own.

She bends down, opens the first zip, and takes Bozy out of his prison for me. I grab him and squeeze him tight. Really, really tight. Just how Bozy likes to be squeezed.

'I know, I can't go back to live there,' I say, looking up at my mom. 'Can I move back in here? I'll sleep on the couch.'

'Course you can move back in here, ma love,' my mom says. 'Course you can.' She steps towards me and kisses the top of my hair. 'And you won't need to sleep on no couch. I'll ask Callum to move his stuff back into Daryn's bedroom.'

'Tell them I'm sorry,' I whisper.

'Tell them yourself,' my mom says. 'You never talk to those boys. Your brothers.'

'I don't talk to anyone,' I say.

'Well, I certainly don't want you talking to that rat bastard anymore,' she says, pointing down at my lap. 'I told you from the very start. He's a rat bastard. A dirty, cheating, rat bastard.'

I shake my head of her talking. And talking. And talking. About him. It's always about him.

Instead, I lift the newspaper from my lap and read its headline again.

MY STORY
Clyde Taylor Reveals All About Elizabeth's Return Home

I wasn't sure what rage was. Not until my mom rang my dad's house this morning to speak with me, yelling that I should go to the local shop to buy *The Sun*. So, I did. It was the first time I'd ever been to a shop. But it is in that shop that I felt what rage was like. For real. I had only ever read about rage in my books before. Now I was feeling it. It didn't make me want to cry. It just made me angry.

I went back to my dad's house with the newspaper under my arm and while him and Winnie watched television, I stuffed the newspaper and Bozy back into my small suitcase and, without saying goodbye to them, I took a train back to Wales. To be with my mom. My mom who never stops talking. And talking. And talking. And talking.

I told him. I told him a hundred times since I got back 'home' that I had no interest in selling my story. I had offer after offer to do interviews when I was found. From TV. Radio. Newspapers. Podcasts. But I kept turning them down. I didn't want to talk to anyone. I wanted silence. I still want silence. I love silence. I want to live inside silence. One TV show in America offered me two-hundred thousand dollars for a one-hour interview. But I still said, 'no'. My dad was angry with me for saying no to that. Really, really angry.

'Take it. Take the fuckin' money, Betsy,' he shouted. 'One hour's work for two hundred grand. Are you mental?'

Winnie was standing behind him, holding her hands to her hips, shaking her head at me.

'Maybe I am mental,' I snapped back at them. 'Probably what living in a basement your whole life will do to a person.'

I think it was the most words I'd ever spoken to anybody since Dod. My dad looked at me, scrunched up his nose, then took another sip from his warm beer before turning back around to watch the television.

My being 'home' had lost its sheen to my dad within months. Mom would tell me over and over again during those months that he had always been obsessed with the limelight. He did interview after interview — to newspapers, to radio stations, to TV channels — when I first went missing. He even took money, then, for interviews. My mom says Winnie was manipulating him back then. I believe that is true. I see it even in the way Winnie looks at my dad. I bet she was the one who told him to cash in for this interview with *The Sun*. They probably got lots and lots of money for it.

'Uuuugh,' I roar again, picking the newspaper up and beginning to rip at its pages. I drop it, in shreds, back to my lap. I hate this feeling! I hate rage. Rage is horrible. Winnie and my dad make me feel rage. They make me feel angry. Really, really angry. They're like the horrible narcissists I read about in my books. Like Dorian Gray. Or Holden Caufield. People who think the rest of the world revolves around them. It makes me wonder why I am not a narcissist. When the world did revolve around me. Literally. I lived in the same room for seventeen years while everyone else was living out in the real world. Yet sometimes I feel I've seen more of the world than my mom or my dad have.

'It's the books,' I keep telling my mom. 'They take you on more adventures than any car can.'

'I'm surprised it took him six months to sell a story on you,' my mom says. Still talking. And talking. About him. 'I bet *The Sun* said to him, this is your last chance of decent money, cos the story's going cold now, you know. No offence,' she says, holding her hand up to me. 'But it's six months since you were found, ma love.' I nod. I'm not really sure what she means by 'no offence', but it's best I don't ask any questions. Otherwise she'll just keep talking. And talking. And talking.

The only two people I ask questions to are my therapists. Dr Moyra Berchall. And Dr Syed Ahmed. Dr Moyra is good. But not as good as making my mind think like Dr Syed does. He understands me the best, I think. He understands that I loved Dod. He gets it. But I'll have to go back talking with Dr Moyra now because Dr Syed is based up in Leeds, where my dad and Winnie live. I'll have to trade him in to move back here. Like I'll have to trade in silence to move back here. But I can't live with my dad. And Winnie. Not anymore. Not after this.

I pick up the shreds of newspaper, rip them further, then drop them to my lap again. Because I don't know what else to do with this rage.

'Whatcha got in this thing, anyway?' my mom says, bending over and zipping the suitcase open even wider.

'My life,' I say.

'Your life?' she says, flipping back the lid. 'Books and underwear,' she says, tossing the few clothes I have onto Callum's bed.

When she has emptied the suitcase of clothes, she begins taking out book after book, slapping them onto the bed. *The Great Gatsby. Harry Potter and the Philosopher's Stone.* The first. And definitely the best. *Moby Dick. Little Women. Matilda.* My favourite Roald Dahl. *1984*, by George Orwell. My all-time favourite...

The hardest decision I ever had to make was choosing which books came with me. I decided on taking books for all ages. All the favourite books I read at different stages of my life.

She slaps my Kindle on top of the *Little Women* paperback and points at it.

'I used to have one of those,' she says. 'But I don't like reading. Bores me.'

I don't say anything to her. I don't ask why she doesn't like reading. I just nod. Otherwise she will keep talking and talking.

She shovels both hands into my suitcase, then begins to pull out stacks of pages. Lots and lots of pages.

'What the hell is this?' she says, pages spilling from her hands. She drops what sheets she can onto the top of the bed, then fingers the very top page.

'*Betsy's Basement*,' she reads.

FOUR YEARS AGO

BETSY

I turn another page over, but instead of reading from the top, I close my eyes and, without thinking about it, I begin to lean fully forward, tipping all the way over until my forehead reaches the bed. Sometimes squeezing my eyes when I'm in this position can stop the headache. Most times it doesn't. But a headache is better than heartbreak. Much, much better.

When I lift my head from the bed, I stare out the window at the whitest stars in the black sky and I try to soak in my favourite sound. Silence. When I hear the silence, I inhale deeply, before placing my finger to the top of the page and glancing down, even though I really don't want to continue reading. I'm too tired. Really, really tired.

I read during the night. I have to. I found my own routine. I sleep when everyone else is awake. And read when they go to bed. I prefer it that way. I prefer the dark. And the silence. I'm more happy now than I've been since I came 'home' a year ago.

Even though I get lots and lots of headaches. All the time. But I'll take the headaches. Because I feel as if I've got my life back. Some of my life back. In pen and paper anyway.

I have spent the last six months reading through these pages, reliving my life in the basement. I know for certain I've read every page at least four times. But the hard work isn't in the reading. Reading's easy. The hard work is putting all one thousand, seven hundred and forty pages in order. And making it all make sense. I joked with my mom not that it took me fourteen years to write all of those pages, and that it would likely take me fourteen more years to work my way through them. I guess it doesn't matter how long it takes. What matters is I'm happier now than I've been in a long, long time. Since the days Dod would walk down the basement stairs with a shiny new book for me. I loved those days. And I love reliving them in these pages.

I glance up at the digital clock beside my bed, my finger still pointing at the top of the page. 05:22. Mom's alarm will buzz soon. She has to be in work for six-thirty, to open the local Tesco. Her alarm buzzes at 5:30am. Bryn works part-time in the pub, pulling pints at the weekends. Callum and Daryn are still at school. Well, they're supposed to be at school. They only go in if they want to. They spend most of their time playing video games in their bedroom, though. They've no idea how lucky they are to have a school to go to. But I don't say that to them. I don't say anything to them. And they don't say anything to me. We just look at each other and nod whenever we pass by in the hallway.

My dad doesn't work. Neither does Winnie. My mom has told me my dad never worked. Not really. He tried to get a career going when I was born, to help out. But he soon packed it in after I went missing.

'You going missing was the best excuse for him to never work,' my mom says. A lot.

I just nod along to whatever she is saying. But sometimes I think I shouldn't be nodding along. Not all the time. I just know from my own eyes that my dad and Winnie love money, but they don't love the idea of working for money. My dad kinda tried to make it up to me after he sold his story to *The Sun*, but I didn't speak to him for a long time after that. One time, when he knocked on the door of my mom's flat, I told her to not let him in. And she didn't. And every time he rang, she told him I would not be coming to the phone. But, when it was my twenty-third birthday two months ago, he showed up at the door again. With a gift. My mom let him and Winnie in that day. And she stared down at the three of us while we sat in her living room as my dad tried to tell me why he sold my story. He said that my being taken wasn't just my story. That it was his, too. That he had lived through it. And he had a right to sell his version of it.

What he was saying kind of made sense, even if my mom was grunting while he was saying it. But what I didn't like was Winnie sitting beside him while he was talking to me, nudging at him to get his words out.

That day, I agreed to see him more often, so I have taken the train to Leeds the last three Saturdays. But I really don't enjoy it. Not just being on a train with lots of strange people but being in my dad and Winnie's small house on a long street. Their silence is a silence that isn't really silent. It's a strange silence. Really, really strange.

My mom hates that I have started visiting my dad again, so she has started to tell me more and more stories about him over the past two months. Different stories. Ones she hasn't repeated to me a hundred times before.

'Y'know, funds that people from all over the world were donating to help try to find you, your dad and that Winnie bitch were pocketing it. Spending it on themselves. Holidays.

Hotels. Alcohol. Good times. I think they were even buying drugs.'

That last bit is a new addition to a story she has told me a hundred times. But I still found myself nodding along. Hoping she would just stop talking. And talking.

She'll come into me in a few minutes when her alarm buzzes. And she'll sit down on the bed beside me and start talking. And talking. About him. She's obsessed with him. She is more obsessed by him leaving her for Winnie Ratcliffe than me being taken from her. His affair hurt her more than my kidnapping. I know it did. I can see it in her when she talks. I can hear it in her words. Dad is all she talks about. It must drive Bryn mad. Then again, she rarely talks to Bryn. Just to me. Constantly. Which is why I have found some happiness in my night-time routine. She will talk to me for half an hour at five-thirty before getting herself dressed for work, then for an hour or two before she goes to bed later... just after I have woken up ready to read through the night.

It does feel strange that I haven't read any book in six months. Other than this one. I would miss reading books if this wasn't the most fascinating book I will ever read... Though that's only when I'm in the humour of reading it. Tonight, I haven't been in the humour. I'm tired. Really, really tried. My eyes are stinging... and they just want to close...

I heave a sigh in and out, then begin from the top of the page, reading my own scraggly handwriting from when I was fifteen years old.

'Ahhh,' I say to myself, reading a diary entry describing the time Dod allowed me up the basement stairs to watch TV for the first time.

I like that I smile when I see Dod's name in *Betsy's Basement* instead of just sobbing tears when I think about him in my head. As if *Betsy's Basement* has brought him back to life for me. I read on, nodding my head, noting exactly where this sheet should go in the final pile. But I keep reading on anyway. Because I love this page. Not just a good day in the basement. But a great day.

Her alarm buzzes before she stirs, groaning as if she is annoyed at another day beginning. As if she hates days. She shuffles in the bed, then gets to her feet, the floorboards creaking underneath her as she stomps towards her bedroom door. There's a pause while she unhooks her dressing gown from the back of the door, then she pulls it open with a creak, walks down the hallway and straight into my room, or Callum's room as it really is, where she yawns and stretches in front of me before sitting herself down next to me.

'D'ye know who I was dreaming of last night?' she says.

'My dad?' I say, sitting my back against the cream wall.

'Yeah,' she says, 'and guess what... your dad was a slithery fox way before I even met him. Did I tell you about the time, when he was only eighteen, that he was arrested for shoplifting?'

I shake my head.

'No, Mom,' I say.

Even though she has told me that story. Lots of times.

8:56

LENNY

'Today *is* the day, yes!' Lenny says.

He places the phone to the top of his gloss-white Ikea desk, then grips both hands atop Jacob's shoulders, the two of them staring down at the shiny black screen with Celina's name flashed across it in a tall narrow font, the digits timing the call ticking upwards underneath.

'I have Jacob here with me. Jacob... it's Celina.'

'Hey Ja-kub,' the phone says. 'You remember me. Of course you remember me. Who else has ever called you Ja-kub?'

Lenny laughs as he bows over his son, trying to make out his reaction. Jacob's eyes look tuned in more than they did this morning. But there's no recognition around his stiff mouth at all.

'Hey,' Lenny says, rubbing his son's stomach. 'You remember Celina, don't you... There it is, that smile. Of course he knows who you are...'

'Of course you do, Ja-kub,' Celina says. 'I need you to come visit me. It's been way too long since I've seen your beautiful face. I want to hug you and Jar-red so much.'

'You know our door is always open,' Lenny says. 'Heck, you've still got your own key.'

'You need to come see me for a change,' the phone says. 'How many times I ask you to come see me, huh?'

'How many times have you begged us to move out there?' Lenny says, smirking.

Celina sniffs a laugh down the phone, causing Jacob to tilt his head.

'Your laugh's made Jacob interested,' Lenny says. 'Maybe we shudda done one of them video calls.'

'Oh, I will, Ja-kub. I will later. Later when your day is over. I'll ring you on FaceTime and we'll talk and talk. Well, I'll talk,' she says, huffing her familiar laugh again. Lenny bows forward, to notice a smile itching on the corners of Jacob's lips, his bucked teeth threatening to show. 'I just wanted to ring your father,' Celina continues. 'To see how he is....'

'I'm fine,' Lenny says, shouting into the phone, rustling his son's hair.

'Of course you are fine,' Celina says. 'You are always fine. Fine. Fine. Fine. All the time.'

'We *are* all fine, aren't we, buddy?' Lenny says, nudging his son.

Jacob tilts his head.

'Yes, Daddy. Yes, Celina,' he says.

'Yeah... that's the boy. You know Celina, course you do.'

Lenny bumps his hip off Jacob, forcing his son to tilt forward; his thick fingers clutching the rim of the white Ikea desk, his bucked-teeth fully showing, his laugh gruff and panting.

'Oh, I've missed that laugh,' Celina says, purring. 'I will

FaceTime later, Ja-kub. I promise. I just wanted to see how your father is doing this morning.'

'I'm fine,' Lenny says.

'Okay, well if you're just going to tell me that you are fine then maybe we should talk about something else?' Celina says. 'Something to steal your mind for some minutes.'

'Go on...' Lenny says.

'I, uhhh... I was reading a paper on Carter-Wiln syndrome last night. I knew it was related to Angelman's, but I'd no idea how closely they are related. It's like a literal cousin of Angelman's. Not a distant cousin like we've assumed for years.'

'Okay,' Lenny says, squeezing at his son's shoulders; conscious he is talking about him, in front of him. He hated doing that.

'Well, in the research I was reading,' Celina continues, 'they said that the severity of the symptoms can simply be slowed by regular outdoor activity, even an hour of walking in fresh air every day can have positive effects. The vitamin D from the sun and the freshest oxygen is vital for humans with these conditions to feel most alive.' Lenny nods his head, then kisses his own lips. 'I could walk them for three hours a day. Every day,' Celina continues.

'I know,' Lenny says. 'I know you could. And I know you would. I wish... I just wish you were here.'

'I wish you were here,' she said. 'I miss them so much, Lenny.'

'All of the Moons miss you, Celina.'

Jacob huffs, then splutters. And his inhales become sharp, as if he is desperate to say something...

Lenny rubs his fingers calmly through his son's thick hair.

'Go on, Ja-kub,' the phone says. 'Do you need to say something? Say what you want to say.'

Jacob's head tilts, the exhaustion of trying to speak causing him to bow, to look down at his webbed feet sprouting from underneath the flare of his red and grey-striped pyjama.

Lenny reaches a hand to his son's stomach, pulsing his fingers slightly in an attempt to reawaken him. But Lenny knows already the moment is gone.

'Thank you for continuing to look into the research papers,' Lenny shouts at the phone. 'We appreciate it. And we appreciate you.'

'It's what I do. It's what I've been studying my whole adult life,' she says. 'The research I read was only small, but that's not to say it is not significant. It was carried out in Germany. In Cologne. The findings were concluded after investigating eighty patients of Carter-Wiln syndrome through Europe. Seventy-five percent of those who took part in the trial showed clear and obvious signs of increased contentment once exercised regularly outdoors in a clean-air environment.'

Lenny nods, then looks down himself at his fur-lined slippers, adopting the same wide-stance as his son standing in front of him. All Moons missed Celina. Whether they knew it or not. Almost as much as she missed them.

Celina had been Jacob and Jared's full-time carer for four years. Up until the middle of last summer, when she returned to her hometown on the fringes of Antwerp to care for her dying mother. Her mother had passed just before last Christmas, but returning to Dublin wasn't to be Celina's next step. Despite her heartbreak. Jared and Jacob meant so much to Celina Pieters. But so, too, did her hometown of Lier—one of Belgium's hidden treats. Lier was coloured by tones rarely found in Dublin. Olive greens and golden rusts lined every street, at every turn, every day, as if it were perpetually peak autumn. Only in the final two weeks of October could Dublin match Lier for warmth of aesthetic. But the aesthetic wasn't the only allure of Lier for Celina. Her family were there. Her friends were there. So, too, was her heart. A heart that had been shredded, with remnants of it remaining in Dublin. In 166 South Circular Road to be more precise—where her two favourite ever patients lived... Or tried to live.

Celina had initially travelled to Dublin for a six-month work trial at St James's Hospital in her final years as an Autism Research major in 2017. But those six months somehow turned into a full year without her seemingly noticing. That was because she had found by then, living in 166 South Circular Road, Jared, and Jacob Moon—two of less than ten-thousand people in Europe who were suffering with Carter-Wiln syndrome. One of only two sets of twins known to share this unique strain of Angelman's disease. Jacob and Jared were, Celina would find, twin sons of an affable private investigator and a strict former teacher, by then retired. Forced retired. Due to on-going bouts of manic depression. The one-year Celina spent in Dublin with the Moon family would somehow transition into four years, but not without her noticing. She *was* noticing. Noticing with her heart straining. She adored Jared and Jacob. She adored the whole Moon family. But she loved home more. She knew home was where her heart beat loudest.

For two and a half of her four years in Dublin, Celina lived in a one-bedroomed flat a half an hour's bus ride away from the Moon family's million-euro Victorian home. But during the COVID pandemic, she was invited to reside in 166 South Circular Road with her two patients and their parents. And for their happiest years, the Moon family were a family of five. Not four.

A crashing stirs both Lenny and Jacob from another silence spent staring at Celina's name in a tall font on the screen, causing Lenny to groan. He swipes his phone from the desk and begins to jog up the creaking steps, taking them two at a time.

'Jared! Jared! What's wrong?' he calls out.

'Daddy. Daddy,' Jared cries from the kitchen.

Lenny chicanes from the top of the basement, stepping into

his brightly-lit kitchen to see his youngest by ten minutes on his knees, stooping.

'No. Leave it!' Lenny screams. 'Fucking leave it! Jesus... I leave you alone for ten minutes, Jared. No! Leave it, Jared!' Lenny skids his phone across the kitchen counter in his rush, then steps forward, ceramic and glass crunching under his foot, to yank Jared by the shoulders, stopping him from picking up the sharpest shard. 'Fuck sake!' Lenny shouts.

'Lenny, Lenny,' the phone spits. 'Is everybody oh-kay?'

THREE YEARS AGO

BETSY

I turn over in the bed when the television turns on.

I already know before looking at my digital clock that it's seven p.m. That's when my mom and Bryn sit down to watch the soaps. I tried to watch one once. Coronation Street. But just once. Stories are better from the page than they are on TV. When Dod would allow me to watch TV with him, we would watch the news. Or quiz shows. Dod loved quiz shows. Which made me love them, too. Even though I only knew answers about books. But if Dod was happy, then I was happy. *The Simpsons* made him happiest. It made him laugh. Him and me. I did see *The Simpsons* on my mom's TV one time last year, but when I watched it, it didn't make me laugh like it used to. It made me feel sad instead. I closed my eyes to try to hear Dod's laugh when I was watching it. But I couldn't hear it. And that made me sad. So I haven't watched *The Simpsons* again. Or any TV, really...

I'm not annoyed that the TV turning on wakes me at seven p.m. I use it as an alarm clock. The start of my day. Or night. To where I live. From seven p.m., up until about ten a.m., when Bryn usually gets out of bed to get a bowl of cereal. That's when I know it's time for me to lie down, get some more sleep. When everybody else is starting their day, I'm usually ending mine. Only interrupted by my mom's visits to my bedroom to talk. And talk. And talk.

I start my day, or night, by holding my finger to the bottom of my Kindle, making it wake with me. The Kindle broke a few months ago. It needed a new charger. Callum got one for me. He had seen that I was sad about the Kindle not working, and when I told him the battery was always low, he came home later that day from school and left a new charger outside my bedroom. Or his bedroom as it really is.

I knocked on the bedroom door that he and Daryn sleep in the next day. The two of them were lying on their beds, listening to music.

'I, uh... I want to say thank you,' I said to Callum.

'No problem,' he said, looking up at me while he lay on his bed.

I had never been in their bedroom before. I'd glanced into it, passing by to go to the bathroom. But I'd never stepped foot inside it.

When the conversation of my broken Kindle came up, Daryn looked like he didn't know what was going on. He didn't know his brother had bought me a new charger. I got to know them a little that day. That's when they both showed me their mobile phones. And all of the 'apps' inside their mobile phones. It scared me. The mobile phone looks like a world I don't want to live in. I don't know why anybody would want to live inside the apps on a mobile phone. Though, I bet nobody would want to live in my world. In one room. Reading. And reading. And reading. And reading.

I visit my dad once every month these days. On a Saturday. To have lunch with him and Winnie in their small house on a long street. He keeps trying to get me to visit his local pub to 'have a drink' with him. But I won't go. I can't. There's just too many people. I tried the coffee shop in Holyhead two times in the past six months. Just to read. But I don't really like being in the coffee shop. Every time a new person walks in the door, and the bell above that door chimes, I get itchy. And scratchy. My elbows start shivering and I can't concentrate on my reading. So it's best I stay on this bed... This boring, cream bed in this boring cream bedroom. Reading.

I touch the screen of the Kindle, and remember I finished a book last night. *The Clergyman's Daughter*. It was a George Orwell book I had heard of. But never read. Not until I saw it would only cost me one credit on my Kindle to download yesterday. So, I did. I downloaded it. And finished it in a day. It was good. Very good. Just not George Orwell great.

I re-read the four-star review I'd left for it last night on screen of my Kindle, then press the backwards button, to go in search of a new read.

Though I really could do with getting back to work on *Betsy's Basement*. I've kind of deserted it. I got bored. Not of the reading. I loved the reading. Especially the first four or five times. I even loved all of the mistakes I found in the reading. But I got bored trying to piece it all together. To make it all make sense... I haven't had as many headaches just reading books on my Kindle as I had when I was working on Betsy's Basement. Which is good. No headaches. No heartbreak. Not any anymore. Not much.

I flick my eyes over my Kindle screen towards the two big bundles of sheets in the corner of my cream bedroom, then sigh really slowly, before looking back down at the screen and pressing my thumb against it, making it blink back to life.

I don't know what type of book to read next. I love all sorts of books. Fiction. Or non-fiction. But it can be painful for me if I read anything that reminds me of Dod. I can still cry thinking about him sometimes. Maybe once a month. Even though it's over two years since he's been gone. Since my whole world turned upside down.

I spend three hours a week with Dr Moyra. But we mostly talk about my life in this bedroom. And not my life in a Dublin basement for seventeen years. I'm not really confused about Dod. I know who Dod is. More than anyone. Even if I did call him Dod when his real name was Gordon. Gordon Blake. It makes me feel really sad when I think that his daughter had gone missing, too. And that that's why he took me. That's why he loved me. Because he wanted me. I haven't got the feeling that anyone wants me since I came 'home'. I miss Dod. A lot. And sometimes I get upset that I will never, ever see him again. Or hear his laugh. But I am happy for the seventeen years I got with him. For all of the books he bought me. For all of the times he made me happy.

A new book cover on the row of books the Kindle is trying to sell to me catches my attention. Making me squint at it. I know that author's name, don't I?

'Frank Keville,' I whisper to myself. I *do* know that name. Don't I?

'*Seventeen*,' I whisper, reading the title.

I click into *Seventeen*, to see a bigger photo of the front cover. That's when I realise why the book caught my attention. There's a photo of me on the front cover. And a photo of Dod. Dod's not in the photo with me. It's two different photos. One taken of me on the day I came 'home'—standing in the room filled with pink and white balloons. Dod looks young in his photo next to me. How he looked when he first took me.

My heart thumps, and thumps while my finger scrolls up the Kindle screen to read the description.

SEVENTEEN

By Frank Keville

SEVENTEEN is the amount of years Gordon Blake held Elizabeth Taylor captive in the basement of his grand Dublin home.

Blake, himself, had been the father of Betsy Blake, a young girl the nation of Ireland went searching for until it was confirmed she had indeed died, most likely by accident on the day she was reported missing.

From kidnapping a four-year-old Welsh girl to replace his daughter, through to leaving his home in his will to a struggling private investigator, took Gordon Blake seventeen years.

In this tell-all biopic by award-winning journalist Frank Keville, Blake becomes human. The darkest side of human...

I slap my hand to my mouth. Then, my fingers shaking, I take my hand away from my face and stab at the book cover. But the book won't download.

'Damn it!' I say, pressing it again. And again.

I don't have enough credits. But I have to read it. I *have* to read it. Now!

'Mom,' I shout, swinging my legs off the bed. 'Mommmmmmmm!'

I rush out of my bedroom, race down the hallway, and into the loud sound of Coronation Street.

'What is it, ma love?' she says, looking over her shoulder. She reaches for the remote control, pauses the TV.

'I need you... I need you to put extra credits in my Kindle account.'

'Oh Jesus, love,' she says, shaking her head at me. 'Not now. Corrie has just started.'

She turns back around, pointing the remote control to the TV.

'No, Mom!' I shout. 'I need you to put three more credits in my Kindle account. I have to read this book. I have to read it now. It's a book... a book about me.'

9:10

LENNY

'What did I tell you, Jared? What did I tell you!?' Lenny shouts in his youngest son's face. 'Come on. We gotta keep the place clean. Today. Today of all days. I said, when I gave you your breakfast, "Make sure not to leave a mess!"'

The phone on the counter screams another 'Lenny,' but Lenny doesn't notice. Or care to notice. Not when his blood is boiling at this level.

He spins on the spot when he hears the creak of the hallway floorboards behind him.

'Jacob, you shouldn't have left your brother alone. Look!' Lenny points down at the shards of ceramic and glass on the kitchen floor beneath his feet. 'His whole breakfast, all over the fucking tiles.'

'Lenny!' the phone screams.

Only Jacob notices the familiar call of Celina's accent. He shuffles his way towards the phone, but before he gets there, he is wrestled by his father, skinny arms wrapping around his wide shoulders.

'Oh, I'm sorry,' Lenny says, sobbing, 'C'mere...' He drags Jared towards his twin brother, so all three Moons can embrace in another hug; another hug in which their father is apologising for losing his cool.

'Lenny. Ja-kub. Jar-red.' The phone calls out. But the Moon boys are now falling against the cupboards, sliding down them, until all three are seated on the cold rectangle kitchen tiles, gripping each other tight, Lenny's shoulders vibrating.

'I'm so sorry. You two mean everything to me,' Lenny sobs, kissing both boys on top of their thick, black hair. 'I'm so sorry for shouting. And cursing. And...' He squeezes them both, then sits more upright, to try to take both boys' faces in. Jacob holds his father's stare for a beat, before blinking away. Jared's stare is transfixed on the veiny design of the kitchen tiles.

'Hul-ho!' the phone spits.

Lenny stares up at the counter, then gulps before patting both boys' backs, helping them rise a little from their slouched position. When the weight of his two boys lifts from his lap, Lenny stands, then walks to the kitchen counter and swipes up his phone.

'Celina,' he says, his voice weak, his tone dull. 'I am so sorry you had to, uh...'

'It's oh-kay, Lenny,' she says. 'I understand. Today... it's a... it's a big day. You will be stressed. I bet the boys are stressed, too. Of course they are. Deep inside them, they will know. They will know what today is. They just can't get those feelings to the surface. That's all. You are all stressed. Of course you are. I should have... I should have flown over to you today. Today of all days.'

'Oh will you stop,' Lenny says, tutting, 'you blaming your-self. When it's me. It's me who should be apologising. I never speak to them like that, Celina. I don't. Maybe two or three times. I just... I just...'

'I know how hard it is, Lenny,' Celina says. 'Just hang up from me. Go clean the mess in the kitchen, give those boys a hug from both you and then me. Tell them how much you love them. And how proud you are to be their father. They'll hear it. And feel it. They'll feel it deep down.'

Lenny palms the phone against his heart and stares down at his two boys still sat on the cold tiles of the brightly-lit kitchen. He holds a hand out to Jared, to pull him up, while Jacob scrambles to his feet by himself, gripping his thick fingers to the curve of the kitchen countertop for support.

'Hey, you three, take care. I will FaceTime later, okay Jakub. You and Jar-red be ready for me before you go to bed, and we'll talk then... oh-kay?'

'Okay,' Lenny says, staring at her name on the phone, 'bye, Celina.'

When the screen blinks to black, Lenny bows his head, allowing the punch to land in his gut. Again.

'I'm so sorry, you two,' he says, clawing his hand into each of his sons' stomachs, tickling them.

Jared smiles, a little. Jacob remains still. Still and sombre. Staring down at the vein in the tiles.

Lenny claps his own hands, once, as he swivels on the spot, glass, and ceramic crunching under foot. Then he bends down and begins to pick up the mess Jared had made when he had innocently tried to bring his breakfast plate to the kitchen sink because he had remembered daddy said the house needed to be clean today. Of all days.

While Lenny is pinching at shards, palming them into his right hand, he hears a crunch behind him, ceramic and glass crackling.

'Hey,' he says, holding his hand to Jared. 'You're standing on it. In bare feet. Lift your foot, lift your foot.'

Lenny holds his arm to the back of Jared, while he tries to lift his son's leg. And when Jared's leg stiffens to an outwards stretch, Lenny brushes down his son's thick, leathery soles, noticing there hasn't been a cut. A tiny graze. But no cut.

'Be careful,' Lenny says.

'Where's Mammy?' Jared asks, holding the stare of his father. It was unusual Jared would hold Lenny's stare.

'She's coming home soon,' Jacob says from behind his brother. 'Remember?'

'Exactly,' Lenny exhales. 'Which is why we gotta tidy this kitchen.'

TWO YEARS AGO

BETSY

I knew as soon as I read the first two sentences that every word in *Seventeen* would be a lie.

Blake by name. Bleak by nature.

I knew what bleak meant. Bleak is a theme in almost every great book I've ever read. Bleak means cold and miserable. Dod wasn't cold and miserable. He was all the light and shine I've ever had.

I could feel rage, reading *Seventeen*. Especially the first time I read it. I would roll my fists into a ball and slam them down onto the bed hard.

Frank Keville was guessing. Sensationalising. That's what he does for his work. Sensationalise. I knocked on Callum and Daryn's bedroom door one evening and asked them to check on their mobile phones to find out who Frank Keville was. He's a crime news reporter. Writing for all of the different newspapers in Ireland. Glamorising crime. Sensationalising it for entertainment. Which is exactly what *Seventeen* does. It sensationalises. I left the book a one-star review. I wasn't the only one. Others left one-star reviews, too. But it was annoying to see lots give it five stars. The book paints a picture of me being held captive for seventeen years. But I wasn't. It says Dod starved me. He never did. That Dod may have molested me. He never touched me! That Dod made me call him Dod because it sounded like Dad. More made-up nonsense. That Dod used me as a slave. An outright lie.

Seventeen is all about a man who didn't really exist. Gordon Blake. Gordon Blake is bad Dod. But Dod was good Dod way more than he was ever Gordon Blake. Which makes this book mostly a lie. A three hundred and ninety page big, fat lie.

I've read *Seventeen* six times on my Kindle. Twice in paperback. I bought it in paperback, too, when I got enough Amazon credits, so I could write notes in it. Before I had even made those notes, I had written a letter to Frank Keville. Callum told me the journalist worked at Independence House, and that he could drop a letter to that address for me the next time he was in town. I wanted to write to Frank Keville to tell him how wrong his book was. To point out how much he exaggerated every sentence in his book. Only my mom stopped me from giving the letter to Callum. And tore it up instead.

I take a deep breath, then rattle my fingers against their door. Again.

I get no answer. So, I wait. And wait... Their television is turned up so loud that they can't hear me. I knock again. Harder... Nothing. So, I creak the door open. And when I step foot inside, I see that they are playing a game on their TV, tapping away at buttons on a remote control. Three of them.

'Ahhhhh,' their friend shouts, staring at me, then jumping back in the bed.

'Sorry,' I say, stepping backwards.

'Fuckin' hell, lads, she frightens the shit out of me...' the friend says.

'Calm down, Snoz,' Callum says, punching his friend in the arm.

I swallow. While I stare at Daryn. Daryn squints back at me, holding his remote control up as if he is still playing the game.

'What is it, Betsy?' he says.

'I, uh... I need a favour.'

Daryn and me had rarely spoken. A nod or a 'hello' in the hallway is all we ever got through over the past three years. Up until a few months ago. When my two brothers saw how upset I was by *Seventeen*. I think it was the first time Callum and Daryn felt I was in pain since I came 'home'. Up until that point, I was just their scary, ghost sister who had stolen one of their bedrooms.

I was raged by so much of *Seventeen* that they could see the rage inside me. In lots of different ways. It was the quotes from people in Dod's life who didn't know the real him that made me feel angry the most. They couldn't have known him. Not the real him. They only knew bad Dod. Not good Dod. His ex-wife got closest to who he really was. Michelle Dewey. She is quoted in the book as saying: "Gordon was a very decent and loveable man when I first met him. But his life fell apart when Betsy went missing. His heart went missing with her. Then his head went missing. Then his body. He became aloof. He lost his daughter. Then lost himself. Then lost me. Then lost his friends. His business... I always felt sorry for him; for his aloofness, for his loneliness. But now we all know why he was aloof. Why he wanted to be alone. We all know what he was hiding..."

She turns the heat up on him then, saying he had 'a fierce temper and liked to be in control', but she is only talking about Gordon Blake. Not about Dod. She can't be talking about Dod. Dod is the guy she married. The 'very decent and loveable man' she first met. That's who he really is. I should know. I spent more time with him than she did. They were only together six years. Me and Dod had had eleven years more than that. That is why the book is called *Seventeen*. Literally.

The only other person in the book who had anything nice to say was Lenny Moon. He was the private investigator who had been left a note on the day Gordon died that said I was in the basement. Whereas everyone else quoted in the book was eager to lie about how evil Gordon Blake was, Lenny said, "my thoughts when it comes to this case are always about the welfare of Betsy Taylor. I hope she is living her best life in her new life." I like that he said that. He also said he felt sorry for Gordon. That he knew that there was a good man inside him somewhere.

But Keville himself had nothing nice to write. He gave Gordon a nickname. 'Desperate Dad'. He gives all of the people he writes about nicknames. It's one of the ways he sensationalises his stories. It shouldn't be allowed. You should only be allowed to write the truth.

Keville mentioned in the book that he approached me for comment. And that I turned him down. I was really angry at that because that was another lie. Until my mom told me that it actually wasn't a lie at all...

'Well, he did call to the flat one day,' she admitted. 'I told him you were not interested in talking to him. That you are not interested in talking to anyone. And you never would be.'

'Mom!' I said, moaning at her. Feeling like one of those spoiled characters in my books, like Jo March, or Tom Sawyer.

Or Katniss Everdeen. 'You could have at least told me,' I said. It felt strange to moan. As if I was being naughty. And I am never naughty.

'Why?' my mom said, staring at me. 'I knew your answer would be 'no'.'

I huffed. Like Katniss Everdeen does. Then I rolled my eyes. Like Jo March does.

'Listen, Betsy,' my mom said. 'I knew you were going to tell your own story. Your own way....' She paused and smiled at me. 'You were telling it. You were working hard on *Betsy's Basement* back then, but you've barely... barely picked a page up out of the corner of your bedroom in months. That's why I ripped up the letter you wanted to send to Frank Keville. You don't need to worry about his book. You've got your own book to write.'

I snapped out of my Katniss Everdeen huff and hugged my mom. She was so right. I didn't have to write a letter to Frank Keville. I had a book to write.

I began to work on *Betsy's Basement* the next night. And then every night. Of every day over the next six months. I got back into my routine. Working while everyone in the flat was asleep. Editing. Redrafting. Rewriting. Until finally, just five minutes ago, I stabbed my final full stop to the final sentence of the final paragraph, in the final chapter...

Their friend inches forward on the bed, staring at me with his mouth open. I've seen him a couple of times, walking through the hallway into the boys' bedroom, where they play games on their TV for hours. And hours...

'Sure, what favour you need?' Daryn asks, putting his remote control down.

'I, uh...' I look around their bedroom; at the two skinny beds lined up against the walls; at their big screen TV; at their black curtains pulled all the way across their window, blocking the day light. I like that. Blocking out the daylight. 'I, uh... need you to check something on your phones for me,' I say.

'Sure,' Callum says, standing up and walking towards me, slipping his phone out of the back pocket of his jeans. 'What you want me to check, Betsy?'

'Can you, uh... can you do a search, please, about how to get a book published?' I ask.

9:20

LENNY

Lenny's cell phone continues to glow and vibrate against the kitchen counter while he vacuums the remaining splinters of glass and ceramic from the tiles. Most of the mess had been binned while the twins were taking their first steps up the stairs to get washed under their father's order. Lenny knew that by the time they got to the top of the stairs, they were likely to have forgotten why they had climbed them in the first place. Well, Jared certainly would. With Jacob, it depended on the day.

When Lenny releases his finger from the vacuum trigger, he hears, through the silence, a knowing creak, and smiles to himself, knowing the twins didn't quite make it fully up the stairs by the time he had cleared the mess.

In the remaining silence, the phone glows, and buzzes against the kitchen counter again, causing Lenny to tilt his head backwards so he can swear into the bright-white ceiling.

'Fuck me,' he whispers, kissing the cuss from his bottom lip.

It's not necessarily the incessant buzzing of the phone that is riling Lenny. It's the swearing at his boys. He just can't help himself. Sometimes it all gets too much, that swearing almost becomes a necessity. As if his blood triggers at a certain boiling point and a switch clicks, causing him to spit cusses at his innocent sons.

Even knowing that Jared and Jacob can't access their memory banks readily, these episodes leave a scar on Lenny's chest. This morning has been the ninth time in the past seven months he has lost his cool with his boys. All nine scars continue to burn him.

The Moons have tried alternative care since Celina headed back to Belgium, but nobody could quite get near the high bar she had set. They trialled two other full-time carers before opting to send Jacob and Jared to regular classes every day instead; classes that Lenny can work his investigative practice around. Jared and Jacob attend a stretching class at ten a.m., every morning. Then in the afternoons they spend two hours, five times a week, at an autism speciality teaching school at St Michael's Community Centre. The class, however, is ill-fitting for Jared and Jacob, for it is attended, mostly, by four- and five-year-old children nowhere as far along the spectrum as they are. But the twins' inclusion in this class gifts Lenny the time he needs to focus on work. He loves his job. It pains him not to be able to offer it more of his time. But it doesn't pain him as much as leaving the twins with a carer they haven't quite connected with.

Jacob and Jared wouldn't be going to any classes today, however. Nor would Lenny be doing much work, save for instructing two separate contacts to check two separate houses his instinct is telling him Alan Dennings may be holed up in. Today would be a different day. A day Lenny had been dreading for quite some time.

He stabs a finger at the phone, ignoring the list of missed calls, and stares at the time. 9:26 a.m.

'Shit,' he says. 'She'll be here in half an hour.'

He stuffs the vacuum cleaner into the mess of all-sorts under the stairs, then races up those stairs, in time to see Jacob and Jared turning the knob on the door of the main bathroom.

'No!' Lenny shouts. 'C'mon, I told you when I sent you upstairs, not the main bathroom. It's always the small bathroom next to your bedroom, you know that! You have to know that by now!'

He looks up to the tall ceiling of the landing and opts to close his eyes firm, rather than swear.

The twins pivot and shuffle towards the small bathroom slowly, with Jacob beginning to unbutton his red and grey-striped pyjama top as he goes. When Jared notices what his twin is doing, he mirrors him, and by the time Lenny joins them in the cramped bathroom, both of their pyjama tops are slip-ping off their long arms. Lenny sits on the closed toilet seat and yanks at Jared's flared pyjama trousers, exposing him with a flash. Jacob pulls down his own trousers and steps out of them, before turning around and sliding the shower door open. He steps on to the tray, shivering, while Lenny turns to the sink, to twist the diamond-shaped tap on before feeling for the water to turn warm. Once it has, he grabs for a light-blue sponge and holds it under the running water.

'Okay, Jared, watch how Jacob does it,' Lenny says as he pushes the sponge against Jacob's torso, before swishing it in circles as if he were polishing a car. 'Lift your arms, Jacob,' he says as his son reaches towards the lifeless shower head. Neither twin likes the shower. They've always been washed by sponge. Warm water. A squirt of all-in-one body wash. And a sponge. A blue sponge for Jacob. A yellow one for his brother. 'Good man,' Lenny says as he sweeps the sponge downwards, wiggling it against Jacob's nether region, turning his face away as he squeezes, padding the sponge around his under carriage. Lenny turns back around, drowns and squeezes the sponge with the warm tap water until the suds are no more, then pivots back, to repeat all of the sponge's movements on Jacob's body, cleansing his son's underarms and under-carriage of soapy bubbles.

When his body is as clear as his father's patience can last, Lenny turns to the radiator to where he had been heating two fluffy, cream towels, removing one. He spreads it wide open and without prompt Jacob steps out of the shower tray and into the towel's warm embrace, his bucked teeth grinning.

'Okay, your turn, Jared,' Lenny says.

Jacob helps his brother to step into the shower tray and spins him around, so his expressionless face is staring outward toward his father, seeing but not watching him take out a yellow sponge and holding it under the warm water. He barely moves as Lenny runs the sponge across his torso. Jared never moves when he is getting washed. Not even when he is getting his nether region scrubbed, the way Jacob sometimes can.

When he is washed of all of his suds, Jared steps into a warm embrace of a fluffy, cream towel, too, and both boys stand there in the cramped space, wrapped like burritos, while their father rids the bathroom of its untidiness. He even goes so far as showering the suds away from the bottom of the shower tray today. Something he rarely does. But today, of all days, the house has to be pristine.

'Right,' Lenny says, slowly pivoting in the cramped bath-room, 'Let's get you dried.'

He stabs a finger against his phone to check the time. Again.

'Shit,' he says.

He thumbs the red circular alert bubble in the bottom corner of his screen, and realises he's had eight more missed calls since the last time he checked. Two more from Sally's father. Two more from Barry and Eleanor. And one each from four other members of his and Sally's inner circle.

He's disappointed, but not surprised, to note none of the missed calls are from Celina. He already knows her name won't be among the twelve text messages he has received so far this morning that he has not yet opened. That's because Celina never texts. She hates texting; feels it too cold a replacement for interaction.

Lenny stretches between his motionless, wrapped-up sons and snatches at the knob of the small bathroom door. When he pushes it open, he has to shepherd Jacob and Jared to spin around and walk out to the squared, carpeted landing. Sometimes Lenny takes in the satisfying smirk on Jacob's face when his cold feet touch that carpet after his morning wash, but not today. Today, Lenny was too preoccupied to notice Jacob's bucked-toothed grin.

If Lenny likes any space in the house, it's this space. The squared landing. If he could set his office up here, he would. He hates working down in the basement; as if he can feel the chilling breaths of the girl who was once held captive down there.

Lenny has felt different levels of discomfort for a range of reasons since moving into 166 South Circular Road some five years ago, despite the luxuries it has offered him and his family. Part of that discomfort comes down to the girl who once lived in the basement. But most of it comes down to the fact that both the twins' condition and Sally's condition worsened inside the confines of this grand old home.

He can enjoy the comfort, if not the ambience, of the living-room, and the soft relaxing breaths he takes on the carpeted landing when he can afford the time to stop and think. But every other room tends to run a chill down his spine. 166 South Circular Road is not like his old house in Tallaght—where he used to live before he inherited this home. That house may have been only one-third the size of 166, but he sure does remember laughing in those tight rooms more than he ever has in this old home.

He turns to Jared first and begins to slap down his body, patting the towel into the crevices that get most wet. He then whips the towel from his youngest son, scrunches it up to get into the harder-to-reach areas, before tossing the towel aside, leaving Jared standing in front of him, naked. Naked and cold.

While he is patting down Jacob, Lenny opts to quiz his eldest by ten minutes. To see if he's tuned in today. Today, of all days.

'You know what today is, Jacob? Dontcha?' he asks, squinting.

Jacob remains silent through the process of the scrunched towel weaving back and forward against his groin. And Lenny is forced to sigh out in disappointment at not getting an answer.

'Right, that's you two washed,' Lenny finally says, giving up. 'Time to get you two dressed. Today... you're wearing suits!'

EIGHTEEN MONTHS AGO

BETSY

I look up, scared, when I hear a sizzle coming towards me. Until I notice that the two waiters are smiling, walking towards me, their faces lit up. Then I don't feel scared anymore. When Monica looks over her shoulder, they begin to sing... to me. All of them. And it makes my elbows shiver. They haven't shivered in so long. So, so long.

> '...Happy birthday, dear Betsy....'
> 'Happy biiirthday tooo.... yoouuuuuu...'

I smile at the two waiters, but I don't like it. I don't like the singing. I don't like the attention. Even if it is nice attention.

One of the waiters winks at me as he places the cake slowly down to the centre of the small table Monica and I are sat at, and I am sure I blush the way characters in my books blush. I'm not sure I've ever blushed before. But it sure feels like it... it sure feels like my face is filling with blood.

'Well, blow em out,' Monica says.

The tall sizzling sparkler at the back of the cake burns itself out as I blow at the two small candles at the front, before glancing up at Monica through the smoke. Catching her eye. I'm getting better at looking at people's eyes. I started doing it with my mom a few months back. And then with my dad whenever I would visit his small house in Leeds. Which is really only once every few months. I've tried making eye contact with Daryn and Callum, too. But they don't seem to like it much. They're a bit like me.

Coming to this cafe over the past few months has helped my confidence, though. I wrote two redrafts of *Betsy's Basement* from here over the past five months. Mom came with me the first two times, just so I could get used to going out. She had promised me this cafe is quiet. And it is. The waiter who winked at me works here most days. I like it when he is working. He knows what I like to eat and drink, and he knows that I like to be left alone. In silence. Writing. Most times there are only two or three other people sitting in here. Sipping coffees. Eating brownies. I like the brownies. Not the coffee. I usually just eat brownies with a glass of water when I'm here. But today, Monica has made me order a sherbet lemonade. Because this is a special occasion.

'Double celebrations, today, hah?' she says waving away the candle smoke.

Her accent is pretty in lots of different ways. It's definitely pretty different.

'Hey, guys,' she calls out over her shoulder. 'How's this girl s'possed to eat her cake, just dig her teeth into it, get me a knife, will ya?'

Monica's accent is even stronger when she is giving instructions. I heard that in the four times we spent talking on the phone over the past four weeks. Sometimes, she would stop talking to me, just to roar at somebody in her office. She scares me a little. Even though she says all the right things to me. All the nice things. She says she believes in me. That she believes in my writing. That she believes in *Betsy's Basement* more than she believes in any book she's ever published.

I tut inside my mouth when I notice it is the other waiter bringing the knife, and not the one who winked at me. But that's okay...

'Thank you,' I say to him as he cuts into my birthday cake.

'A quarter of a century old, hah?' Monica says.

I smile my thin lips at her again, and when the waiter places a large slice of cake on a small plate in front of me, I stare down at it, before picking up my fork.

'Thank you,' I say. Again. Because it's all I ever seem to say. He nods, then walks away.

Monica reaches into her bag while I suck cake from my fork. I love cake. It reminds me of the times Dod would surprise me on my birthday.

'Here ya go, girl,' Monica says, slapping the paperwork onto the table. She licks her finger, then turns the first page while I wash my tongue around my mouth, catching the crumbs that got away. 'As I promised,' she says, stabbing her finger at all of the zeros.

Monica did promise all of the zeros. Monica has promised a lot. She promised she would be here. Today. With a contract for me to sign. And when I told her that it was going to be my twenty-fifth birthday on the day she said she would be here in Holyhead, she said, 'Great, well I guess I'm gonna bring some cake, too.' Another promise she has kept.

Monica looks like nobody I have ever seen before. But maybe all American people look different. Her hair is the darkest black I have ever seen hair be. And her top lip is as big as her bottom lip. It's so big, it looks as if it is curling back on itself, back towards her nose. I wish I had full lips like that rather than the thin lips that I've got. Lips that don't smile. Not even when I'm eating cake. Which is my favourite thing to do. I'm not even smiling while eating cake *and* staring at all those zeros. I noticed how big her lips were on the two FaceTime phone calls we had with each other. Callum and Daryn's phones allowed me to talk to somebody in America on a video call. It was so cool. It was even cooler that she was telling me how much she loved *Betsy's Basement*. And how much she thinks she can do for the book over all of the other publishing companies who wanted to get their hands on it. I sent photocopies of Betsy's Basement with a covering letter out to ten publishing companies when Callum and Daryn got all of their postal addresses for me on their phones. Within eleven weeks, I had had calls or letters from nine out of the ten. All offering to publish *Betsy's Basement*. One company, in London, offered me two hundred thousand pounds on the very first phone call I had with them. I couldn't believe it. They said they would give me two hundred thousand pounds before they even sell one copy. They called it an 'advance'. When I told another publishing company in Edinburgh that I had been offered two hundred thousand pounds advance, they told me they would double that if I signed with them there and then. And that they would make it tax free. My head got spinny on that phone call. And I started to feel like I was a character in one of my books again. I guess I kind of was in a way.

Two weeks later, I got a phone call from Penguin Random House. They wanted to give me five hundred thousand pounds, then told me they would see to it that *Betsy's Basement* was the biggest selling memoir of the decade. I couldn't believe what I was hearing on that phone call. I couldn't make any sense of anything. And that was all before America got involved. When everything changed. One of the publishing companies in London had sent a copy of *Betsy's Basement* to what they called a 'sister company' in New York City. That's how I would meet the woman with the darkest black hair I've ever seen, and a top lip that curls back towards her nose. Monica Witch. The editor in chief at Harris & Witch—the third biggest publishing house in all of America. She said, on that first phone call, that she would blow all other publishing companies out of the water if I signed with her. 'I'll get you more zeros,' she said. 'I promise I will get you more zeros. Tax free, too. You'll get every penny. I promise.' She kept her promise. I know that now, staring at all of the zeros, stuffing another forkful of cake into my mouth. It's not the number of zeros I'm staring at that makes me excited. It's what they represent. The value of my writing. Of all my hard work. Somebody believes in my writing *this* much. Six zeros much. That makes me feel warm. Much warmer than I've felt for years. And years. Not since my days in the basement.

I feel cold at 'home'. I still feel out of place. Even though it's been three and a half years. I heard Daryn shouting at Callum a few weeks ago that he, 'needed to fuck off out his bedroom once and for all.' It made me feel bad. Not just because I knew I was the reason they had to share a bedroom, but because I thought we were friends. Me and them. I thought they finally liked having a sister. They had helped me find the publishing companies' addresses. Then they helped me find somewhere I could photocopy the pages. Then they helped me post the photocopies out. I don't think they hate me. They just hate that I got in their way. They are right to think that. I did get in their way. Literally. I'm not getting in my dad's way, though. I barely see him these days. Maybe three times in the past eighteen months. I still haven't told him about *Betsy's Basement*. Or all of the zeros. Because I know how obsessed he is with money. Dr Moyra has said to me twice that my dad sounds like he needs his own therapist. I agree. I just wouldn't say that to my dad. He wouldn't understand it. I know he wouldn't. I really like Dr Moyra. But I'm thinking of leaving her. I've been with her for most of the three and half years since I came 'home'. But I'm not sure she is going to help me any more than she already has. Writing *Betsy's Basement* was all the therapy I've ever needed. It made me think everything through. It made me answer all of the questions Dr Moyra had been trying to get me to answer.

'So,' I say, placing my fork back down to the side of my empty plate, then washing my tongue around my gums again. 'What will the front cover look like?' I ask.

'Oh,' Monica says, rolling her eyes. 'Don't worry about that. Your job is writing. My job is publishing. A book cover designer's job is designing book covers. They'll know what to do.'

I nod my head, then take a sip of my sherbet lemonade, staring down at the zeros again. The lemonade is nice. But I'd rather water.

'Biggest deal we've ever handed out,' Monica says, stabbing her fingers against the zeros. 'One million pounds. You deserve every penny of it.'

I nod again, placing my lemonade back to the table.

'Thank you... for believing in me,' I say.

'I believe in your writing,' Monica says. 'Your story blew me away. It blew me away this much,' she says, still fingering the zeros. 'Listen..' She folds her arms and leans forward. 'Publishing is a slow business. It could take another year, maybe even eighteen months for us to get *Betsy's Basement* out into the world. But when we do, we're gonna sell millions of copies. All over the world!'

'Wow,' I say, tapping my fingers against my glass of lemonade.

'Millions?'

'Millions and millions,' she whispers back in her pretty accent. 'We're gonna run a huge marketing campaign just before the book comes out, Betsy... and I know exactly where we're gonna start...'

9:46

LENNY

Lenny pulls the two loose strands of the bow tie until the knot tightens against Jared's Adam's apple, then slaps a hand to each of his youngest son's cheeks.

'There ye go, buddy. You look deadly.'

When Lenny steps out of the way, so Jared can take in his own reflection in the tall mirror, the sight of him in his two-piece jet-black suit with crisp white shirt and silver bow-tie almost causes him to show his teeth. But not quite. Jacob had already grinned his bucked-teeth upon seeing his reflection ten minutes prior. But Jared didn't mirror him as he stared at his own reflection because too much time had passed since he'd noticed his brother's smile.

'Now, lemme do this,' Lenny says, swivelling towards the chest of drawers in the twins' bedroom. He pinches a squared red bottle from the top of the chest, then swivels back, pushing his thumb downwards, spraying Jacob's neck with a once popular Hugo Boss scent.

'Daddy! Daddy!' Jacob shouts, squirming away.

It's Jacob's fury that finally causes Jared to show his teeth; his smile growing wide and wet until his father turns the spray on him.

'Daddy! Daddy!' he cries, spinning away, his hands held up.

'You both smell delicious,' Lenny says, dropping the bottle back to the top of the chest of drawers. 'Right, time for me to get dressed. Dang it!' he says, slapping a palm to his forehead. 'I forgot to brush your teeth, didn't I? I shudda bloody brushed your teeth before I got you into those suits, huh?'

Lenny puffs a laugh out of his nose, then notices that Jacob is giggling into his hand behind his brother.

'You laughing at me?' Lenny says. 'You laughing cos I forgot to brush your teeth before I decked you out in your fancy suit? I'm not quite as clever as Mammy or Celina, am I?'

Lenny, smirking, spins on the spot, then strolls out of the twins' bedroom and across the carpeted landing where he forgets to stop and breathe before pushing his own bedroom door open. The path from the boys' bedroom to his own bedroom was a path well-trodden. So much so, the carpet was beginning to fade in a straight line from one door to the other. He allows his dressing-gown to slip from his skinny arms, then hangs the oversized hood to the hook at the back of his bedroom door before stepping his way out of the H&M boxer shorts he wore yesterday and slept in overnight while walking towards his chest of drawers, from where he removes an identical pair of boxer shorts and steps into them. In one choreographed move. A move he carried out most mornings without even noticing. There's a slight fumble as he snatches a pair of black woollen socks from his drawer before slipping them over his narrow feet. And then, when he steps to the right, he slides the door of his standing closet open with a swoosh of his hand, before holding that hand to his hip while he takes in his hanging clothes, huffing... He can't decide what to wear. Not today.

'Fuck it!' he says, reaching for a navy roll-neck jumper and then a pair of navy trousers. 'It's neutral, in'it? Navy.'

He steps into the trousers, then pulls the woollen jumper over his bald head before ridding it of its rolls by patting down his torso, tugging it taut at the end. 'It doesn't fit,' he whispers, sucking his belly in, 'as well as it used to'.

He shovels his hand into his hanging dressing-gown pocket to scoop out his phone, then stabs his thumb at the screen to see there's only been one missed called since he last checked. From Barry and Eleanor. Again. Sally's sister and brother-in law. They had by now rang a total of six times this morning. One call shy of his father-in-law's total.

Before dropping the phone back into his pocket, he checks the time. Again.

9:52.

'Shit,' he says.

He paces towards his chest of drawers, reaches for his clear moisturiser, and then begins to smother his bald head in wet gel until it dries, gifting his scalp a momentary glow. He takes his red-squared bottle of Hugo Boss from the top drawer and squirts himself eight times; four shots to each side of his neck. Then he rubs his hands together, to signal that he's fine. He looks fine. Semi-formal is fine. For him. For today.

He paces towards his bedroom door with a rush, and then, upon pulling it open, is stopped dead in his tracks, his socks sticking to the carpet as he sucks a sharp inhale to the back of his throat.

'Jared! No! What the... WHAT. THE. FUCK?' he screams, stomping his woollen socks across the squared landing. 'I bloody told you. How many times I fucking told you?'

He tugs Jared by the collar of his crisp, white shirt, skipping his son's webbed feet from the cold tiles, back to the cosy carpet. Then he collapses to his knees, gripping Jared tight around the waist, panting. When he looks up, he notices Jacob is standing in the centre of the squared landing behind them, staring into the main bathroom.

'Jesus, Jared,' Lenny says, squeezing his son's waist even tighter before clambering back to his feet, yanking the door of the main bathroom to a slapping close. 'What were you doing? What were you thinking?'

Jared slowly looks up from his webbed feet, to meet the eye of his twin. But he doesn't say anything. He doesn't have anything to say.

Jacob, maintaining eye contact with his brother, raises his hand up towards his own mouth and opens his lips to a grin, before vibrating the hand in front of his smile.

'Brushing your teeth?' Lenny mumbles. 'You were going to brush your teeth?' He stares back up at Jared, then engulfs him in a tighter squeeze, wrapping his arms around his waist. 'Because I said I forgot to brush your teeth before... right?' He leans off his son, then motions with a wave for Jacob to join their embrace. Which he does. He takes three thudding steps forwards to grip his father with one long arm and his brother with the other, the three of them leaning inwards, their foreheads touching. But rather than breathing in the moment, Lenny is feeling the immediate self-punch to the gut he always feels moments after losing his cool with his boys.

'Fuck me,' he sobs, spraying the cuss from his mouth. He swipes a hand up to his face to catch the tears. But it's too late. Both cheeks are wet. He cries into his hand, then sniffs up his nose before stretching both arms across the shoulders of each of his sons, squeezing them tighter.

'I'm sorry,' he sobs. 'I'm so sorry. Let's go brush your teeth in the small bathroom, next to your bedroom, huh? We always use that one now. It's always that one.' He kisses Jacob on the cheek, then turns to Jared to offer him the same peck; hoping it will kiss away their memories of him swearing at them in a rage. Again. For the second time today.

When the three-way embrace splits, Lenny pinches the cuff of his navy polo neck jumper and brings it to his face, to wipe away the wet. When he feels his cheeks are dry enough, he swallows before sucking in a heavy breath and exhaling it with a sigh. He stretches an arm across a shoulder of each of his sons again, and begins leading them towards the small bathroom... When their feet stop dead at the same time, planting into the carpet as the trill of the doorbell pierces up the stairs at them.

'Holy shit!' Lenny says. 'She's here...'

THIS MORNING

BETSY

I tried to breathe in the air as soon as we got off the plane. But it didn't work. Because there were too many people around, and it made me uncomfortable. As if I couldn't breathe. It didn't help that Monica was walking fast the whole time. She was always far ahead of me, and it made me wish I had said 'yes' to my mom when she said she should come with us. At least she would have stayed by my side around the airports. Even if she would have talked and talked and talked and talked. There were just too many people at the airport for me to enjoy breathing in the air. The worst part was where all the bags were going round and round. I didn't like it. I didn't like the smell. I didn't like the heat. I didn't like the sound. The chatter, chatter, chatter.

When we got outside to where the man picked us up in his big, black car, I tried to breathe in the air again. Thinking it would bring me back. Hoping it would bring me back. But it didn't. The air didn't smell like anything I remember. When I was driving over here in the big, black car I assumed that as soon as I saw the front door that it would take me back. But it hasn't. Not even as Monica is holding her finger against the doorbell.

Monica had proven to be way too loud for me to be around too often. She is very bossy. And shouty. Not with me. But with other people. Like her assistants. Or her staff at Harris & Witch. Or waiters at the cafes or restaurants we would meet at. She is the boss everywhere she goes. So, I mostly speak to her over FaceTime when we needed to talk. Which isn't that often. Not really. She would usually just invite me to a restaurant or call me on FaceTime to tell me, 'Slight delay, Betsy. But we should be ready to go next month.' She has said that to me seven times over the past eighteen months. But that 'next month' she was always talking about was last month. And we are finally here. Two days until *Betsy's Basement* is released into the world. I'm excited about that. Not nervous. All of the nerves leading up to the launch have been about this single moment right here. Ever since Monica told me this was the first place we had to go to market the book.

It's when the door pulls open that I'm taken back. It's the brown floorboards along the hallway. They make my head spin. Almost immediately. I squint through the darkness of the hallway, past the man who opened the door, to try to make out the big brown door at the end of the floorboards. But I can't make it out. Not yet. It's dark in there. Really, really dark...

'So you must be Monica,' the man says, causing me to blink away from the shadows of the hallway.

'And you are Betsy,' he says, extending his hand towards me. 'It's my absolute pleasure...'

He looks older than he did in the newspapers after I was brought 'home'. More than five years older. And he's really small. And skinny. And pale. And he has no hair. But he has kind eyes. Really, really kind eyes.

'Mr Moon,' I say, placing my cold hand inside his warm hand. I started shaking people's hands the first time Monica brought me to Harris & Witch's office in London last year. London was scary. But I liked the faces I met in the office. Faces of all different colours. From all around the world. I felt happy after meeting them. That's when I started going to restaurants and not just my local cafe. I've been to five restaurants now. One time on my own. That was scary. But I think I will do it again. I prefer to be out of my mom's flat. I much prefer being inside a cafe than inside my cream bedroom. Or Callum's bedroom as it really is. I'm not scared in the cafes anymore. In restaurants, I can be scared. A little bit. Sometimes. Especially that time I went on my own. But I want to keep doing it. I think I do, anyway.

'Lenny,' he says, 'Call me Lenny, please.'

'I...I,' I say, stuttering, letting go of his hand.

'Hold on!' Monica nudges at my elbow. 'Let me...,' she says, taking her phone out of her purse, then holding it up before stabbing a finger to the screen, 'film all this.'

When Lenny takes a step out from his doorway, and onto the small garden path next to me, I squint down the wooden floorboarded hallway again, trying to make out the big, brown door at the end of it... When. I suck in a breath and slap my hand to my chest. Frightened. Scared. I almost scream. But I don't. Because that will scare the two boys who have walked off the bottom step, frightening me. They're dressed in suits. Fancy suits As if they're going to a ball.

'Okay, and action,' Monica says, nudging at my elbow again. 'Go on,' she whispers. 'Walk in.'

I blink my eyes away from the two boys in fancy suits, then I breathe in and out really slowly before stepping one foot back inside 166 South Circular Road. It's warm inside. Already. As warm as Lenny's hand felt when he took mine inside his. I sniff through my nose when my second foot steps onto the brown floorboards, and suddenly my whole body feels warm. Even my insides. I can smell it. I can smell the air! I try to not look at the two boys as I slowly step past them. I squint, instead, into the shadows, making out the shape of the big brown door at the back of the hallway. Until I can see it. Really see it! The door hasn't changed. Not one bit. I feel warmer. Much, much warmer. So, I take another step forward... then another, slowly, holding my hand out, desperate to touch the bronze knob.

'Okay, great,' Monica shouts from behind me. 'Now, Betsy...'

'Yes?' I say, blinking myself away from the bronze knob, then spinning to face her, thinning my already thin lips.

'Eh... lemme past you,' she says, walking backwards, still staring at her phone, 'you go outside the front door again, and I'll film you coming in from inside, hah? That way we get shots of you entering the house from behind for the first time in five years, then entering face-on for the first time in five years...'

I don't say anything. I don't say, 'but it won't be the first time in five years when I do it again, because I've already just entered for the first time in five years.' I just walk out, back out of the house, back out the front door of 166 South Circular Road. Back into the cold.

'Okay, Betsy, and when I say 'action' I just want you to look sombre and walk towards me... Holy fuckin' Jesus Christ!' she screams, clutching her chest.

She spins on the spot and starts breathing heavily. Really, really heavily.

'Please...' Lenny says, pacing inside, 'Please don't frighten them.' He steps towards the two boys dressed in suits and hugs both of them. 'These are my sons, Jared and Jacob. Jared. Jacob,' he says, pointing his finger out the door towards me. 'This is the girl I was telling you about. This is Betsy. Betsy who used to live here.'

I stare at the two of them, but they don't stare back at me.

They are staring down at the brown floorboards beneath their feet instead. They look odd. Very, very odd. But everyone looks odd, I guess. I bet I look odd to people. It is probably best to not care what you look like to other people. None of the best characters in my books care about what they look like to other people.

'Jeez Louise,' Monica says, still holding her chest. 'Is... is there somethin' wrong with 'em?'

I sigh slowly, and hold my eyes closed, because I know that is not a nice question to ask. She does that a lot, Monica. She asks questions that can make me feel like I'm blushing sometimes.

'They, uh, they have a rare form of Angelman's disease,' Lenny says.

'Wow,' Monica says, staring at them. 'What's that?'

'It's, uh... it means they're very high up on the autism spectrum. Really high up. That's the best way to say it in layman's terms,' Lenny replies.

It makes me stare at them even more. *Autism*. Christopher Boone had autism. In *The Curious Incident of the Dog in the Night Time*. And Boo Radley in *To Kill a Mockingbird*. Two of my favourites.

'Anyway, okay,' Monica says, looking the boys up and down before turning to me. 'You ready, Betsy, I'mma record you coming in, hah?'

I nod.

'Sure,' I say.

'Rightie... okay. And, action,' she shouts.

I step into the warmth. Again. For the second time in five years. I swallow hard, then I start walking. And walking. Walking past Lenny. And his two sons dressed in fancy suits. Then past Monica with her phone held high, pointing down at me. Walking... walking... until I can reach my hand out and it finally touches the bronze knob of that big, brown door. It feels hot. Not just warm. But hot. Comfortably hot. I hold my breath while I twist my wrist to open it.

'And cut!' Monica shouts. I swallow again. The bronze knob still hot in my hand. 'Great stuff, Betsy, you looked really sombre walking in there. Uh... okay, lemme go down to the basement before you, hah?' she says, 'film your face as you're walking down?'

I don't say anything. I just take three big steps back until I'm standing in front of Lenny and his two boys dressed in fancy suits.

When Monica snatches the big brown door open, I look away. I glance over my shoulder instead, to stare at the stairs the boys had just walked down when they frightened me. It makes me think of the time I snuck up them. And found newspapers all about a missing girl I thought was me in Dod's bedroom. Dod was right. It wasn't me in the pictures. I wasn't Betsy Blake. I wasn't Dod's daughter. Not his real daughter. So many memories of being upstairs flows through my mind. And suddenly the warmth in me feels warmer. And warmer. I almost smile my thin lips staring at those stairs. But I stop myself. In case Lenny and his two boys are looking at me. Best I keep my smile inside myself.

'Okay, come down now, Betsy!' Monica shouts up the steps of the basement.

I suck in another breath, then I look at Lenny and thin my already-thin lips at him before turning to face the open door. I take one step forward, then another, and I can see down the steps I used to stare at a thousand times a day...

10:19

LENNY

She touches the wall. Again. Then the ceiling. Again. That's what she did when she first walked down here. She told Lenny, when she first touched the ceiling, that it had just become a memory inside her head that Dod had been painting the basement ceiling this exact colour. 'On the day he died,' she whispered to herself. Lenny wasn't sure if he was to hear her whisper.

'I, uh, I liked the colour he was painting it,' Lenny said, keeping the conversation alive. 'So, I kept it. It's a nice light blue. Makes it airy.'

'That's what I thought,' Betsy whispered, still stroking her fingers against the wall. 'That light blue would look airy. Like the sky.' She spun all of a sudden, to look Lenny dead in the eye, her own eyes glistening. 'Most of the time I was down here it was just grey,' she said.

'Why, this sure is the most I ever did hear you talk, Betsy,' Monica said, flicking her eyes over the screen of her phone.

Lenny had noted in the twenty minutes since he had first shaken Monica Witch's hand that she sure had a habit of sounding inappropriate at the most inappropriate times.

He held his eyes closed in frustration at yet another ill-timed, curt Monica-ism before opening them to glance back at Betsy, catching her eye before she turned away to touch the walls again.

She had just spent the past ten minutes posing awkwardly for the screen of the iPhone Monica was now lost inside. There were videos shot of Betsy coming into the house for the first and a second time. Then a video of her walking down the basement steps. Shot twice from the same angle. Just because Monica wanted 'two shots in the bank'. There was even a video of Betsy lying across Lenny's desk—showing where her bed used to lie. Monica then took photos in all of those places before Betsy began touching the walls again.

'Think we got some great shots,' Monica says, staring at her phone. 'It's a pity it's all been repainted and kitted out like some sort of office. But.... these photos and videos will fly viral. It'll work great in marketing. We'll roll this stuff out through our socials over the next forty-eight hours and it'll explode.'

'That's right,' Lenny says. 'Just two more days until your book comes out, Betsy.'

'Hmm, hmmm,' Betsy says, looking around at Lenny bash-fully, then back at the wall again.

'I can't wait to read it,' Lenny says.

'I actually have a copy for ya,' Monica says. 'Left it in our hulk of a car outside, didn't I? Gimme a sec...'

Monica races up the steps of the basement, stirring the boys standing still in the hallway. Lenny peers up the steps, to see Jacob tapping Jared on the shoulder before whispering something into his ear. He always felt his heart grow when he would witness the older twin comforting the youngest with a whisper.

'Shall we meet Monica upstairs?' Lenny poses to Betsy.

She continues, silently, to rub at the sky-blue wall. Then she does something Lenny hadn't noticed her do as yet. She smells her hand.

'Sure,' she says, without turning around.

'In yer own time,' Lenny says, before he begins to climb the steps, staring at his twin boys above him as he inclines. When he reaches the top, he spins round to peer down at Betsy, to see her still touching the walls.

'Here y'are, Lenny,' Monica says, pacing back through the hall door. 'Betsy signed it for you.'

She slaps a hardback copy of *Betsy's Basement* into Lenny's hand, and he stares down at the front cover to see a picture of Betsy as she looks now, holding a photograph of Betsy when she was just four years old. The photograph that was used all over the news when she went missing.

'Thank you, Betsy!' he shouts down the steps.

He notices her remove her hand from the wall, then slowly look up at the four faces glaring down the steps at her. She shrugs her shoulders, then, slowly, and uncomfortably, swivels and walks the length of Lenny's desk towards the steps before climbing them. Slowly. Like a ghost.

'S'why you guys look so fancy?' Monica asks, fingering Jared's bowtie.

'Please,' Lenny says, gripping her elbow, 'don't touch them. They're... they're shy.'

'Sorry,' Monica says, holding her hands up, causing Betsy to glare at her just as she joins them on the floorboards of the hallway.

'Eh, Jacob, Jared, why don't you go upstairs, into the small bathroom, get some toothpaste on those brushes, huh?'

Jacob nods at his father, then taps his twin on the shoulder before leading him towards the main stairs. They grip the bannisters with their thick fingers, then climb them with a slow shuffle, huffing and puffing. While Lenny and Monica watch them navigate the first steps, Betsy swivels her head over her shoulder, to stare down the basement steps...

When the twins look as if they're comfortable, Monica decides it an appropriate time to ask one of her inappropriate questions.

'Why they dressed so smart?' she whispers.

'We, uh...' Lenny says, his eyes blinking. 'We.... are off to a mass.'

'A mass?' Monica says, sniggering. 'On a Thursday? You Irish!'

'No, it's, uh...' Lenny hesitates again, staring down at the brown floorboards beneath his feet, his eyes blinking rapidly. 'It's my wife's anniversary. We lost her. Two years ago today.'

Betsy turns around immediately, slapping a hand to her chest. Monica swallows. Hard.

'Oh my gawwwd,' she says, her American accent broad. 'Am I sorry to hear that?'

'It's okay,' Lenny says, shaking his head.

'Cancer, was it?' Monica asks, without hesitating. Causing Betsy to hold her eyes closed. Again.

Lenny scratches at the stubble of his shaved head, just above his ear.

'No,' he says, softly, 'she, uh... I, uh...' He scratches at his stubble again. 'I came home one day with the twins to find her in our...' he shifts his feet on the floorboards. 'She was in the bath. Her eyes opened. She had taken too many pills. On purpose. Then got into a warm bath.'

'Oh my,' Monica offers.

Betsy's hand remains slapped to her chest, her bottom lip popped open.

'I bet you didn't need us coming here today,' she says, softly... 'Of all days.'

'It's okay, Betsy,' Lenny says. 'I couldn't say no to you coming back here for the first time in five years, could I?'

Monica blows out her cheeks, then removes her iPhone from her trousers pocket and brings it towards her face, her fingers and thumbs tip-tapping against its screen. Betsy takes one step forward, reaching out to touch Lenny's shoulder. He looks down at her hand, then into her eyes. They look heavy. But not dead. As if there was life still inside them, dying to be lived.

'Kay,' Monica says. 'Let's leave this man and his boys alone, Betsy. We gotta get you back on a plane soon anyway. Take you back home.'

'Home,' Betsy mumbles, her hand still slapped to Lenny's shoulder.

Monica slips her iPhone back into her pocket, then holds her hand to Lenny's other shoulder.

'Thanks, Lenny Moon,' she says. 'We got what we needed. Pity the basement was painted all fresh, but I'm certain the images will make their way around the world over the next few days.'

'Great,' Lenny says, motioning to open the front door, allowing both women's hands to drop from his shoulders. 'I'm glad you got what you needed.'

He pulls the door open.

'Kay, Betsy, let's go!' Monica says.

She places her hand inside Betsy's and leads her out of the front door of 166 South Circular Road. Back out to the cold.

Lenny takes two steps backwards, hooks an arm around his bottom banister, and stares up the stairs.

'Hope you two are in the small bathroom!' he shouts. 'I'll be up in one minute to brush your teeth!'

He paces to the open front door, to where he waves at Betsy

glancing over her shoulder at him before she is shepherded by one of the most obnoxious women Lenny has ever met towards the back of an oversized, shiny black SUV parked outside.

Lenny watches and waits so he can wave at the blacked-out windows as the SUV finally drives off, then he closes the door of 166 South Circular Road, before racing up the main stairs, to where his sons have been waiting for him on the squared landing.

'Yis look deadly,' he says, slapping each of them on the chest.

'Come on, let's get those teeth brushed. Then we can get going.'

As he is shepherding them into the small bathroom, he slips his mobile phone out of his trousers pocket to note the missed calls he had received in the half an hour Betsy and Monica had taken over his home.

Three missed calls.

Two more from his father-in-law.

And one from.... He sucks in a breath, then stabs a finger to the screen before a ringing tone crackles through the speaker.

'Hul-ho Lenny,' Celina answers, her accent thick. Her tone sombre.

RIGHT NOW

BETSY

Before the big, black car pulls off, Monica already has her phone held up close to her face, tip-tapping her thumbs against the screen.

'This is gonna be the most viral marketing campaign we've ever run,' she says. 'And it's so fuckin' simple. It didn't cost a cent. Genius!'

I thin my lips at her before twisting my chin over my shoulder, staring back at the front door of 166 South Circular Road, to see Lenny waving at me. I wave back. Then I stare through the open door behind him. I want to go back in there, touch those walls again. Feel how warm it is. Smell that air. But I can't. Not now. Not now the driver is pulling the big, black car out, his indicator click, click, clicking...

I rub my sweaty hands together, then feel disappointed when the front door to 166 is out of sight. Really, really disappointed. My chin sinks into my neck.

'We're probably a lil early for the airport,' Monica says, her face still in her phone.

'Hmmm, hmmm,' I say. Just to let her know I heard her. Just to be polite.

'Flight isn't for three hours. Probably could have stayed in there a little longer. Got more photos.' I lift my head, and turn to face her, which makes her look away from her phone. 'Uh.. would you have liked to have stayed in there longer, Betsy?' she asks.

She annoys me sometimes. Irritates me. A bit like my mom irritates me. Talking. Talking. Talking.

'It's okay,' I say. When what I really want to say is, "Of course I would have loved to have stayed in there longer you absolute fff...." I can't even cuss inside my own head. Even though I want to. I want to cuss out loud. Really, really loud. Like some of the best characters in my books do.

When the driver stops at a red light, I try not to think of all the cuss words I could scream at her. But cuss words keep coming to my mind.

The click-click-click is giving me a headache. I shouldn't be feeling like this. I shouldn't be sad. Not when everything I have ever wanted is about to happen to me. Literally. In two days' time, I'll be a published author. A published author of a best-seller, Monica says. I know she gives me headaches. And makes me feel embarrassed sometimes. But she has kept every promise she ever told me she would keep. So, instead of being angry with her, I sit back and hold my eyes closed so that the headache might go away, just as the driver takes off again.

'This is a fuckin' great shot,' Monica says.

When I open my eyes, I see she is holding her phone towards me, showing me a photo of me lying across Lenny's desk with my eyes closed.

'Yes,' I say, nodding my head. I glance away, out the side window, watching the big, red-brick houses flash by...

'We'll use the footage of you walking down the basement for the first time for the main promo, but I think we'll ask all the newspapers to use this photo of you lying across the desk, hah? It says something don'tcha think?'

'Hmmm, hmmm,' I say, still staring out the window.

I tend to say 'hmmm, hmmm,' when I don't know what else to say. It's a new word I made up. I only ever use it when I'm with Monica. Or with my mom. When they are talking and talking and talking.

'Yeah, that's what we'll do,' she says, continuing, the American accent I used to think was really pretty now irritating me. 'I'll ask all the newspapers to use this as the main image. You look at peace in it. Did you feel at peace down there? Down in the basement?'

'Kinda,' I say, shrugging my shoulder, still watching the houses flash by.

'Good girl,' she says. 'You're so at peace. Don't think I'd be at peace if I'd been through everything you've been through.'

'Hmmm, hmmm,' I say.

'I can't believe Lenny let us into his house today,' she says, 'when it's his wife's anniversary. How sad.'

'Hmmm, hmmm,' I say, closing my eyes, my headache niggling me.

'The fact that he let us do our photoshoot today. Of all days.'

'Hmm, hmm.'

She continues. Talking about Lenny. Then about the photos and videos she's going to use for different marketing campaigns... But I don't listen. I can't listen. Not anymore. I keep my eyes closed, tightly, sighing my exhales onto the window. I'm irritated. Not just by Monica, but the fact that the car is still moving...

'That right, hah?' she says, raising her voice.

I pop my eyes open and turn my face towards her.

'Is what right?' I ask.

'Jeez, Betsy, are you not listening to me? Your book is coming out in two days. You should be listening to me.'

'I, uh...' I say, shaking my head.

'I said,' she says, 'you've got three interviews tomorrow with podcasters in the states, then four interviews in total on Friday. Two with American networks. Two with UK-based networks. *GMB* in the morning. Then *The One Show* on Thursday evening. You'll be calling in from home for all interviews. You told me you just wanted to do these interviews from your bedroom, right?'

'Hmmm, hmm,' I say nodding.

She tried, for months, to convince me that I shouldn't call in the interviews, that I should appear in the actual studios for them. But I didn't want to. It didn't feel right. I'd be better on my own. In my bedroom. With Monica hooking me up to her laptop.

'You sure say 'hmmm, hmmm' a lot,' she says.

I know she's disappointed that I'm not appearing in the studios, but it didn't affect the contract she put to me eighteen months ago. I'm still getting every tax-free penny she told me she would get me if I signed with Harris and Witch. On the day the book comes out. Every zero she pointed at.

'Okay, then on Friday,' she says, continuing, 'on the day of release, we've got those interviews you did last week with journalists appearing in all the magazines and newspapers. But the main marketing will be the social media. With these images. These videos. Our publicists are predicting we'll sell a million copies globally by midnight Sunday.'

'Hmm, hmm,' I say, staring back out the window.

"Hmm, hmm', is all you can say to selling one million books in one weekend?' she says.

'No,' I say, sitting more upright, re-facing her. Again. 'It's just you've told me that a few times already.'

She raises one of her eyebrows. Maybe I'm irritating her as much as she's irritating me.

'Okay, well, I'll make sure to not repeat myself around you, girl,' she says. I'm not sure if she's serious. Or if she's joking. It's hard to tell with Monica. She picks up her phone, stares at the screen again, then starts tip-tapping her fingers against it. 'So, I know I spoke to you about how we can roll these out through social media, but what I think we should really do is—

'No... stop!' I say, holding my hands to my face. 'Stop. Stop. Please stop. Stop everything. Stop! Stop! Stop!'

10:33

LENNY

Lenny places one hand on Jared's chest then helps his son's head to tilt slightly forward with the other.

'Okay... go,' he says.

Jared spits the toothpaste out of his mouth, leaving a string from his gums to the sink that Lenny has to mop up with the palm of his hand, before running that hand under the tap and bringing it to his son's mouth again, swiping and wiping away the mess.

After Lenny dries around Jared's mouth with the facecloth, he wrings his own hands in it before sucking a deep inhale, then roaring it out, causing an echo to bounce off the four tiled walls of the small bathroom.

'Daddy!' Jacob complains, holding his hands to his ears.

'Sorry, buddy,' Lenny says. 'Just a big sigh before we go. Okay, are we ready?'

Jacob nods, before Jared mirrors him, slowly.

'Right then, follow me,' Lenny says, scooping the lit phone from the radiator, then pacing out of the small bathroom, across the squared landing and down the stairs, lifting the phone back to his ear.

'Sorry about all that, Celina,' he says, 'Just trying to get the boys out the door.'

'No. I am sorry for ringing again, Lenny,' Celina says. 'I just… I just couldn't get you three out of my mind. Not after hearing how you spoke to the boys earlier—'

'Look, I'm sorry about that,' Lenny says. 'I'm sorry you had to hear it. My patience just… it just snaps every now and then. Just for a minute. That's all.'

'Len-ny,' she says. Slowly. Her accent thick. 'I know you'd never hurt Ja-kub and Jar-red. I know. Come on. I know you are not that man.'

Lenny attempts to hide his sigh as he stares back up the stairs he had just descended, the phone gripped to his ear.

'Come on, lads, we gotta get going!' he shouts.

'Lenny, listen to me,' the phone says. 'You need me. The boys need me. They need this air. This fresh air.'

'Celina, I… listen, I gotta get these guys to this mass. Their grandfather will throw a hissy if we're late, especially as I've not been answering his calls all morning. They've all been ringing me. As if they think I need to take fifty calls this morning of all mornings. I'll see them all here… at the mass. Isn't that enough of the melancholy?'

'What is melancholy?' Celina asks.

'It's, uh… it just means sadness, Celina.' He sighs again. Heavily. 'LADS! Come on, let's go!' he yells.

'Lenny, just listen to me for one moment,' the phone says. 'You can't go out to work trying to find other people's children and then come home to try to find your own. That is two full-time jobs that nobody in this world could do by themselves. You are losing your patience. You said it yourself to me.'

'I'm not just losing my patience. I'm losing my mind.'

'Yes!' Celina says, cheering.

'Huh?' Lenny says, squinting. 'You're happy I'm losing my mind?'

Lenny's face frowns as soon as he looks up at his twin boys shuffling down each step slowly, side-on, gripping the bannisters tight with their thick fingers.

'No. I feel happy you have finally stopped saying, 'I'm fine',' the phone says. 'I know you're not fine, Lenny. You can't be fine. Not doing all this by yourself.'

'I can't give up looking for missing children,' Lenny says, gurning at his sons' slow progress.

'I am not asking you to give up looking for missing children,' Celina says. 'I know how much doing that work means to you. All I am asking is—'

'I can't,' Lenny says.

'You can't what?'

'I can't just move to Belgium, Celina,' he says. 'I'm from Dublin. We're Dubs.'

'Ja-kub and Jar-red's lives would be more fulfilled in a clean-air environment,' Celina says.

Lenny holds his eyes closed in frustration; not frustration at Celina, frustration with his entire situation. His career. His family. His life. His grief. His lethargy. The fact that the twins take four minutes to decline the bloody stairs.

When they finally reach the bottom step, he opens his eyes, feeling a sting in them.

'Len-ny,' Celina says. Her accent broader. 'Talk to me...'

Lenny steps into the living-room, grabs his yellow puffer jacket from the armchair he had draped it over yesterday, and slips his arms into it.

'The two of yiz look deadly,' he says, stepping back into the hallway, ignoring the phone. Jacob offers a toothy grin to his father as he shuffles forward, but Jared didn't notice his older brother's smile and so didn't mirror him this time.

'Len-ny, please,' the phone persists. 'If you lived here, you could take up any number of those missing children cases in Europe. Base yourself here, right in the centre of Europe. Do what you love doing best. Find missing children. I would look after Ja-kub and Jar-red while you—'

'Celina,' Lenny says, sighing the name out of his mouth, 'you've said all this to me a dozen times. I can't just up and leave... I can't just give up everything I have, to move to another country. It's complicated. A move like that is way too complicated for us right now.'

'No, it is not,' she says.

'Look, I gotta go,' Lenny says pulling his front door open. 'Celina, I appreciate all you are saying. I know you want what's best for Jacob and Jared and you will always want what's best for them, but—'

'I am saying what is best for all three of you,' Celina says. 'Not just Jared and Jacob. You need this fresh air as much as they do... You cannot go on losing your patience with your sons the way you did this morning.'

'Twice this morning,' Lenny admits sombrely, staring up and down the South Circular Road, still gripping the phone to his ear.

'Twice this morning, Len-ny. Really?' the phone says.

'Look,' Lenny says, 'I gotta go. The mass starts in twenty minutes and it's a twenty-minute drive.'

'Len-ny, please... please. Please just say you'll think about it.'

'I've always thought about it,' Lenny says. Not hesitating. 'Since you first mentioned it. But... listen, I gotta go.'

He pushes an exhale out of his nose, then presses a thumb to the screen of his phone, ending the call with a whimpering beep.

'Come on, you two,' he says, stepping outside, feeling the welcome warmth of the spring sun.

The twins shuffle slowly out of the house, gripping their father's forearm for support while stepping over the lip of the door frame.

While each of the twins scrape their clunky shoes along their small pathway, Lenny pulls the door closed and locks it with his key, his temples lightly vibrating with a mind way-too-full.

His phone buzzes in his pocket, sending a familiar tone his way. A tone he is always eager to attend to. Not a ringing tone. Nor a text tone. An email tone. A work tone.

He stabs at his screen again, opening the email.

Got him!

You were right, Lenny. Alan Dennings was in his friend's da's house out in Salthill. Spot on again.

Lenny smiles to himself, then turns around to find the twins are already out the gate, shuffling their heavy frames down the footpath. Lenny palms his phone back into his pocket and strides after them.

'You first,' he says, placing his hands to Jared's shoulders.

He guides his youngest to the car, then places his hand into the pocket of his yellow puffer jacket and pinches at the key ring, forcing Jared to cover his ears from the piercing double beep.

'It's okay, Jared,' Lenny says. 'Here y'go, buddy.' He pulls the back door open, then holds his hands to the top of Jared's head assisting him into the back seat. Lenny then stretches over him, clicking his seatbelt into the catch.

When he spins back around, he notices Jacob blinking away from his stare. Hiding his eyes from his father.

'You okay, Jacob?' Lenny asks.

Jacob doesn't reply. Which isn't unusual. But even so, Lenny slams the door behind him, leaving Jared inside the car alone, then takes a step towards his eldest-by-ten-minutes.

'You okay, son?' he tries again.

Jacob continues to stare down at the concrete beneath his feet... remaining as still as he can.

'I'm proud of you,' Lenny says. 'Very proud of you. I know you know what day today is. I know you do.'

Jacob's eyes blink and he licks all around his lips before coughing.

'Jacob. You know what today is, don't you?' Lenny pushes.

'Mammy died this day,' Jacob says.

Lenny creases his lips, then wraps his arm around Jacob's head dragging it towards his own chest.

'She loved you, Jacob. She loved us all. That's why she couldn't keep going. She wanted what was best for us.'

He leans away from his son, to see if his son's eyes are as moist as his own. But they're not. They're dry. But they look tuned in. More tuned in than they've been any time today.

'Why do you pretend to Jared that Mammy is always on her way home, buddy?' Lenny asks with a whisper.

Jacob says nothing, and his eyes flicker downwards.

'Son?' Lenny says, prodding.

Jacob remains still.

Lenny gives up, exhaling with a sigh again before leading his son to the other side of the car.

When he reaches for the handle to pull the door open, he is stopped, by Jacob grabbing at his wrist.

'I tell Jared Mammy is coming home because he cries every time we tell him she is dead.'

Lenny's bottom lip pops open, and he goes to speak... only he can't. Jacob squeezes at his father's hand and pulls the back door open, leaving Lenny lost for words as he climbs into the back seat, pulling his seatbelt from over his left shoulder himself and then clicking it into the catch.

'You are a great big brother,' Lenny whispers, leaning into Jacob's face, slapping his cheek with a wet kiss.

When Lenny stands back upright, a tear falls from his eye and he swipes at his cheek with one hand while slamming the door shut with the other, before staring up and down the South Circular Road again.

'Right, Lenny. Let's get your game face on,' he whispers to himself. He'd been dreading this day since this day last year. Sally's family haunted Lenny. He felt an air of guilt around them that he knew would never distinguish.

He swipes his hand across his face again, then paces to the other side of the car where he climbs into the driver's seat in front of Jared.

'Right, we'll put some Harry Styles on when we get motoring, okay? And you two, no singing this time, yeah?'

He eyeballs the rear-view-mirror with a grin but gets nothing in return. As he is looking at Jacob, he wonders if his eldest could recall the conversion they just shared sixty seconds prior. Probably. Probably not. With Jacob, it depended on the day. Today he seemed fuzzy. As if he was tuning in, then tuning back out.

Lenny turns the key in the ignition, then flicks his indicator down before stepping on the gas, easing the nose of his car out of its parallel parking space. He squints up and down the South Circular Road, to find all is clear, then presses on the gas, clicking up the gears as he motors away, the red-brick urban homes of Dublin's inner city fading to olive green and golden rust fields. A perpetual autumnal scene.

Suddenly, he snaps from his daydream, punching his foot to the brake, causing the twins to lean forward, then slap backwards into their chairs.

'What the fuck?' Lenny says, snatching the driver's door open, stepping out, then slamming it shut behind him. 'What the hell, Betsy?' he says, striding to the front of his car. 'I almost killed you... You ran straight out in front of—'

'Lenny!' Betsy talks over him, her eyes wide, her hands wringing, her breathing sharp. As if she's been running. Running for her life. 'I came back to ask... to see if... Lenny, I want to offer you one million pounds for your home...'

To be continued...

FROM INTERNATIONAL BESTSELLING AUTHOR

DAVID B. LYONS

WHATEVER HAPPENED TO SOFIE LE SAUX?

BOOK THREE OF THE LENNY MOON NOVELLA SERIES

Read the first chapter of
Whatever Happened to Sofie Le Saux?
Now....

600,000 people are reported missing throughout Europe every year. Half of which are children.

That means, more specifically, that 5,700 children go missing throughout the continent every single week.

Or..

815 children

every

single

day.

LENNY

11:30

Lenny's never felt comfortable with heights. Which is why the calm usually offered by the floor-to-ceiling windows as he paces the carpeted corridor of the fifty-second floor of The Empire Building has been failing to attract his glance.

When he stops at the glass elevator shaft, he allows a cringe to trickle its way through his jaws, before stabbing a finger against the flashing digital arrow pointing downwards. He squints to soak in his reflection in the glass while the elevator rises with a distant whizz, noticing he is wringing his hands. Again. With a huff, he shoves his hands into the deep pockets of his yellow puffer jacket, then spins on the spot to find himself staring down at the maze of rust-orange rooftops five hundred feet below...

And from not being able to glance at the view as he walked, he finds himself enamoured by it; engrossed particularly by the sight of the St. Vitus cathedral, standing proud amongst the web of rust-orange roofed homes. His fixation erodes the cringing... but only momentarily.

The cringing began as soon as he had strode out of the penthouse office of Prague's tallest building, the silence he left in that room screaming at him.

He squints through the rust-orange roof tiled houses, towards the grey roofed tiled houses of the suburbs in the distance, noting how jam-packed every street of Prague truly is. When the elevator arrives with a swoosh behind him, Lenny kisses his lips at the dramatic view, then swiftly swivels his slight frame inside the glass box. And when he pushes at the button marked 'zero' he feels a self-punch to the gut, reigniting the cringing. Taking him down as swiftly as the elevator.

'I'm a fucking eejit,' he whispers to himself as he descends in the glass box. 'A fucking eejit.'

He replays his answers over and over again in his head, wincing at every hesitation and stutter he can hear. Until that's all he can hear.

To distract from his own embarrassment, he slips his phone out of the pocket of the yellow puffer jacket he wore over his brand-new navy suit and holds his thumb above the screen... waiting... and waiting...

When the glass box finally reaches ground zero, and the doors slide open with a swish, Lenny steps into the marble lobby and immediately stabs his thumb to the screen, before lifting the phone to his ear.

'Hul-ho.' She answers before one ring tone has completed; her accent thick. 'How d'it go, Len-ny?'

'Ugh,' he scoffs, scratching the stubble above his ear. 'I mean, I made a fuckin' ass of myself, didn't I, Celina? I was stuttering like a prick... and blinking. Blinking all the time. And my hands kept wringing under the desk. But it was a glass desk, so they could see my hands. I mean...'

'Oh, Len-ny, I bet you did great. You're just being hard on yourself.'

'Uuugh, I dunno,' he says, his voice dejected. 'It's just, y'know, when they ask questions and stuff, I'm just not that quick at answering them, am I? I need time to think things through. I've never been good like that.'

'I bet you did great, Len-ny,' Celina says. 'Why are you always being hard on yourself?'

'How are the boys?' he asks, chicaning the conversation.

'They're great, Len-ny. Of course they are. They've been smiling every day since you moved here. They're smiling now. I will send a photo...'

'So, they're not missing me?'

'No,' Celina says, pushing it out with a giggle. 'I bet you miss them more.'

Lenny stops pacing, his pointed leather shoes screeching against the stain-marble tiles of The Empire Tower's extravagant lobby.

'I miss them so much,' he says. 'Is that weird, Celina? It's been, like, what twenty hours? How can I miss them so much?'

'It's not weird, Len-ny,' she replies. 'It's the first day you've been away from them since... since Sally died. Yes, Len-ny. I can tell they miss you. But they will be so happy when you get home tonight. They're out in the garden smiling, Len-ny. They're smiling. That's all we can ever ask of them. That's all we can ever ask of anyone.' Lenny holds his eyes closed, already feeling the warmth embrace of the hugs he will engulf his boys in when he arrives home. 'But it is not important how we are feeling here,' Celina follows up with. 'It is only important how you are feeling right now, Len-ny.'

'Uugh,' he says, shaking his head. He begins pacing again towards the grand entrance he had walked through an hour previous, his chest thumping with anticipation. 'I'm grand. A little knackered. I didn't really sleep last night, y'know? The hotel bed was just... different. And I just kept thinking of the interview. Over and over again.'

'What questions did they ask you?' Celina asks.

'Ahh, mostly about my experience. They asked about the Betsy Taylor case a lot.'

'And?'

'I dunno. I'm confused about that case. Always have been. Everyone seems to think I solved it, don't they? I didn't really. But I'll take it... I guess it got me in here in the first place, didn't it?' He stares around the grand marble lobby as he continues to stride across it, the sheen of wealth flickering and blinking back at him. 'I'm just... I'm cringing that I stuttered and hesitated so much. And I was blinking. I barely stopped blinking, Celina. And my hands... Jesus.'

He slaps a palm to the top of his bald, pale head.

'I bet they loved you, Len-ny.'

'Oh, I dunno about that,' he says. 'I think I felt a bit intimidated, y'know. It was three grey-haired blokes sitting across a long glass table staring at me, asking me question after question, judging my answer after answer. They were judging me with their eyebrows, Celina.'

'Eyebrows? What are you talking about, Len-ny?' she says with her familiar giggle.

'The main one, in the middle, he had like a thick head of white hair and jet-black eyebrows that pointed downwards. Like upside down hairy Nike logos. He's the chief exec of the PTU. Dr. Chuck Vol—'

A finger on Lenny's shoulder causes him to snap his lips shut, and as he takes the phone from his ear, he swivels on the spot... slowly. Taking in, firstly, the thick mop of white hair in front of him, then the jet-black eyebrows pointing downwards like two hairy Nike logos.

'Uh, Celina,' Lenny says. 'I, uh... I gotta go.'

He stabs his thumb against the red button on the screen, then gulps. As silently as he can.

'Sorry to disturb your call,' Eyebrows says, a sheet of paper slapped against his silver tie.

'That's...uh, okay,' Lenny says, his eyes blinking rapidly.

'Moon,' Eyebrows says. 'Welcome to the PTU.'

'Huh?' Lenny says, his nose squishing. 'Are you... are you serious? I thought I sounded like a stuttering wreck in that interview—'

'Look,' Eyebrows says. 'You're a terrible interviewee, Moon. But we believe you to be a fine investigator. Besides,' he says, stepping closer to Lenny and lowering his baritone. 'We are shit short of investigators given the amount of missing people, so you could have shat on the glass table in that interview, and we'd still have hired you.'

Lenny shakes his head.

'O-kay,' he says slowly, unsure. He's been unsure of Dr Chuck Volgt from the moment he sat in front of him a little less than an hour ago, glaring at his unique eyebrows. 'It would be an honour to be part of the PTU team.'

Lenny holds his hand out. But Dr Volgt doesn't notice, or pretends not to notice. So, Lenny tucks his hand back into the pocket of his yellow puffer jacket, remembering as he does so that he never took the puffer jacket off for the interview, like Celina had insisted. What was the point in paying two-hundred and twenty euros for a brand-new navy suit when he never got to show it off. He was only bringing the yellow puffer jacket for good luck. But he was supposed to leave it outside the interview room. Not walk in enveloped by it.

'You'll find the People Trafficking Unit a professionally-run organisation,' Dr Volgt says. 'But it's professionally run because its investigators don't ask questions. Not in here.' The beady eyes beneath the bushy eyebrows flicker a little. 'You guys ask questions out there.' He points towards the grand entrance. 'Not in here.'

'Sure,' Lenny says, a smile itching on the corners of his lips, his head beginning to nod enthusiastically. 'When do I, uh... when do I start?'

Dr Volgt slaps the sheet of paper he had been clutching to his chest against Lenny's oversized jacket.

'You start right now.'

'Right now?' Lenny asks, his voice high-pitched as he peels the sheet away from his jacket to stare down at an image of a young girl smiling back at him.

'We believe she was swiped this morning. Will need finding by tonight... Otherwise she's gone, Moon. Gone for good. Sofie Le Saux will be traded before you and I are taking our first bite of croissants in the morning...'

WHATEVER HAPPENED TO SOFIE LE SAUX? IS NOW AVAILABLE...

You can purchase the THIRD book in the Lenny Moon series by using the link below:

https://mybook.to/sofielesaux

If you enjoyed

WHATEVER HAPPENED NEXT?

I would be very, *very* grateful if you could leave a review on Amazon.

My kindest regards,

David

ACKNOWLEDGMENTS

This book is dedicated to my incredible readers. Thank you so much for investing your time and money in my stories. Your support gifts me the autonomy to create more stories for you. I hope you enjoyed this one... I truly appreciate each and every one of you from all corners of the world.

I would specifically like to thank Stardust Book Covers for their fantastic design work on this novella. They had the tough task of bringing a twenty-five-year-old Betsy to life and nailed it. Great work, Nastasia, and all the team at Stardust.

A huge thanks also goes to my editorial team of Brigit Taylor, Maureen Vincent-Northam and my beta readers, Deborah Longman, Eileen Cline, and Hannah Healy.

Your feedback is a gift to me, and I appreciate each and every one of you.